TEXAS TORNADO

☆

Dan Quarles was the big man in Logan. And he had one hundred and fifty hired guns to keep it that way. He put it bluntly to Johnny Canavan, "Get out of Logan—and stay out. Or stay here and be buried."

But Johnny Canavan was a Ranger, a redhead with a low boiling point. He did the only thing a Texan could do . . . he strapped on his six-guns and he rode out to take on Quarles—and *his* gunmen.

Other SIGNET Westerns
by Lewis B. Patten

- ☐ **GUILT OF A KILLER TOWN.** Frank Kaily returns to his home town of Medicine Arrow to find that he was the last reminder of the town's secret shame—and the whole town was eager to kill him. (#P4491—60¢)

- ☐ **POSSE FROM POISON CREEK.** A very unlikely posse including one beautiful woman makes looking for three bank robbers more trouble than County Sheriff Webb Dolan can handle. (#P4456—60¢)

- ☐ **APACHE HOSTAGE.** One man is held hostage by a group of angry Apaches. (#P4220—60¢)

- ☐ **THE TARNISHED STAR.** The sheriff of a western town becomes a drunkard and lawlessness runs rampant until the sheriff's son determines to restore honor to his father's badge. (#P4089—60¢)

- ☐ **DEATH OF A GUNFIGHTER.** Patch had been the sheriff of Cottonwood for 20 years and now he was involved in a struggle for survival—a struggle to keep his job, Claire and his life. A major motion picture starring Richard Widmark, Lena Horne and John Saxon. (#P3840—60¢)

**THE NEW AMERICAN LIBRARY, INC., P. O. Box 999,
Bergenfield, New Jersey 07621**

Please send me the SIGNET BOOKS I have checked above. I am enclosing $_____(check or money order—no currency or C.O.D.'s). Please include the list price plus 15¢ a copy to cover mailing costs.

Name_____

Address_____

City_____State_____Zip Code_____

Allow at least 3 weeks for delivery

The Texan

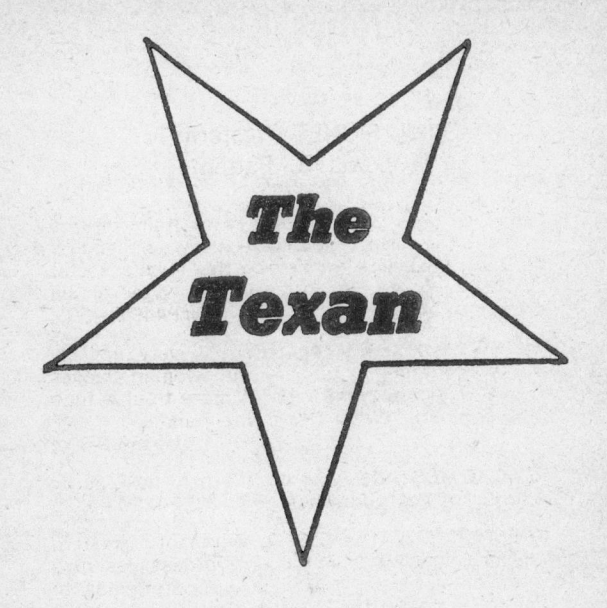

BURT ARTHUR

A SIGNET BOOK from
NEW AMERICAN LIBRARY
TIMES MIRROR

COPYRIGHT, 1946, BY ROBERT M. MCBRIDE & COMPANY

*Published as a SIGNET BOOK
by arrangement with Robert M. McBride & Company,
who have authorized this softcover edition.*

EIGHTH PRINTING

For
Myron and Florence Werner

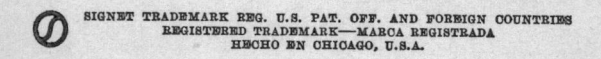

SIGNET TRADEMARK REG. U.S. PAT. OFF. AND FOREIGN COUNTRIES
REGISTERED TRADEMARK—MARCA REGISTRADA
HECHO EN CHICAGO, U.S.A.

SIGNET, SIGNET CLASSICS, SIGNETTE, MENTOR AND PLUME BOOKS
*are published by The New American Library, Inc.,
1301 Avenue of the Americas, New York, New York 10019*

PRINTED IN THE UNITED STATES OF AMERICA

Contents ★

1.	The Side of the Angels	7
2.	Blood on the Moon	15
3.	Canavan Hires Out	23
4.	Quarles Strikes Back	30
5.	Double Trouble	37
6.	Angels with Clipped Wings	44
7.	Quarles's Law	51
8.	Shadows on Horseback	58
9.	Canavan's Return	65
10.	Trick for Trick	73
11.	The Strength of the Weak	82
12.	An Eye for an Eye	91
13.	Canavan Strikes Pay Dirt	100
14.	The Handwriting on the Wall	107
15.	Honor Among Thieves	114
16.	The Reckoning	121

1. The Side of the Angels ★

CANAVAN pushed the faded curtain aside, raised the window and looked down into the street below.

"Uh-huh," he muttered shortly. "So this is Logan, and this is what it looks like the mornin' after the night before!"

He made a wry face when his head throbbed again. However, it was evident from his tone that his first daylight view of the town had not impressed him beyond expectation.

"Yeah," he continued. "Might as well be Silver City or Tonopah, or even Leadville, or f'r that matter, it could be 'most any one o' the hundred or more towns I've been in, f'r all the diff'rence it makes. They're all the same, 'cept f'r their names. They've all got one street, leastways most o' them have on'y one, and sometimes it runs straight but more often it's plumb cockeyed. Still, a street's a street, and the way they figure it, a street makes a town. But f'r my dough, when you've seen one cow town, you've seen 'em all."

His eyes ranged the street below him.

"A street that was once just a trail that b'came a road and fin'lly mushroomed into a street—that's how a settlement b'comes a town. Wonder when it was better off, the way it was in the beginnin', or now?"

There was a restaurant opposite the hotel. Through the lower half of its wide window he could see a counter and a high wooden stool, and to the left of the counter, a table and a couple of chairs. There was another restaurant a bit farther up the street, and a third one near the corner. The place across the street was a bit more dignified than the others. A weather-beaten sign that hung over it read "Restaurant"; the others made no attempt to disguise themselves, neither did they try to deceive prospective trade. Their crudely lettered signs, doubtless the painstaking and painful handiwork of their respective owners, bore the very briefest of legends, the single word "Eats." As an added touch, one "eatery" modestly branded its wares "The Best Grub Anywhere"; the other had a sign over its doorway that read "Your Friends Eat Here. Why Don't You?"

Canavan's eyes shifted back to the "Restaurant." A banner that hung over the upper half of the window informed a nostalgic public that this was the nearest thing to home: this was "Mother Jones' Place." At that moment a tall, gaunt woman with a deeply lined, leathery face, sharp black eyes and thin, tight, colorless lips appeared in the doorway. Canavan's eyebrows arched.

"Wonder if that's Mother Jones?" he mused. "If it is, I'll bet a lot o' pr'spective customers expectin' t' be greeted with a motherly smile take one look at her and hightail it away fr'm there 'bout as fast as they c'n run. I know doggoned well that's what I'd do, and the chances are I'd head f'r that corner saloon and get p'lluted till the picture o' her was plumb gone."

A drunken man with bowlegs that bespoke many years spent in the saddle came staggering down the street. When he came abreast of the woman in the doorway, he halted on unsteady legs that appeared to be functioning separately and independently, turned and looked at her, doffed his battered hat and made an almost tragic attempt to bow to her. She frowned and gave him a hostile stare.

"Get along with you, you bum!" she snapped, obviously unimpressed by his gallantry.

The drunk stiffened indignantly, put on his hat, turned awkwardly and trudged off. He stumbled suddenly, tripped over his own feet and went down on all fours. Somehow, although it required a great deal of disentangling, he managed to get up again and turn himself around.

"Hey!" he yelled in a whiskey-cracked voice. "What's the idea o' pushin' me, huh? Think you own the hull danged street? I'll have the law on you f'r that, see if I don't!"

He straightened up, hitched up his pants and belched suddenly, his eyes almost popping out of his head.

"Ol' hatchet face," he said as scornfully as he could.

"Why, you—!" Mother Jones screamed.

She came bounding out of the doorway with a broom clutched tightly in one bony hand and her full, ground-sweeping skirts caught up in the other. The drunk, recognizing the swift approach of disaster, wheeled and fled for his life. His pursuer gained on him with every ungainly and unladylike stride. She was almost at his heels, with the broomstick now gripped in both hands and raised aloft for one crushing, devastating blow, when he swerved suddenly and, with an unexpected burst of speed, broke away from her and plunged headlong into a nearby alley. Mother Jones swung lustily but wildly, but he was then safely out of range. Frustrated, she panted to a stumbling stop. Angrily and breathlessly she considered for a moment the advisability of continuing the pursuit. Then she apparently abandoned the idea, for she turned and retraced her steps to the "Restaurant." Her lips moved, but judging by the way she gripped her broom, it was certain that what she was muttering was anything but what a mother would have thought, let alone given voice to.

Canavan, grinning, waited for the drunk to reappear. Presently he did. He emerged from the alley slowly and cautiously. He held a wooden box in front of him, evidently to serve him as a shield. When he found that Mother Jones had gone, he tossed the box aside, relaxed, mopped his sweaty face with his shirt sleeve and hitched up his pants. Slowly he plodded up the street, halted when he came to a saloon and went inside.

There were a dozen saloons and cafés within the confines of that single street. The saloons, like the ordinary eating places, made no bones about their purpose in the community's life. The word "Saloon" was emblazoned across their windows in plain letters. The cafés went in for a bit of grandeur and embellishment. There were, Canavan discovered as his eyes ranged over them, very definite and recognizable traces of fairly recent washings on their windows, and that he decided, was probably the distinction between the cafés and the saloons.

The biggest and busiest place in Logan was a café on the far corner. Its huge sign read "Kansas City Café." Canavan winced when he read the name.

"If the slop I drank there last night is what they dish out in Kansas City," he muttered, "I'll sure steer clear o' that town."

He recalled without any too great difficulty his visit to the "K. C." bar the previous evening; the earlier hours of his visit were quite clear. It was after that that he seemed a bit vague about what had happened there. As he remembered it, the place was well crowded. He had sauntered in and stopped to listen to a man at the piano.

"Howdy," the man said, looking up at him. "What's your fav'rite song?"

"Oh, reckon I like 'Prairie Moon' 'bout as well as anything else."

"Awright. Buy me a drink an' I'll play it for you."

"Sure."

Canavan could almost see himself striding off to the bar. When he returned, he handed the man the drink and watched him down it at a single gulp. That was how it all began. Canavan couldn't recall how many trips he had made to the bar. He did recall, however, that he'd finally decided it would be impolite to let the man go on drinking by himself. He remembered that he had bought a freshly opened bottle of whiskey, swung a chair around, seated himself beside the piano player and poured drinks for both of them. Between them the bottle was duly emptied. The rest of the evening was now vague, and considerably headachy too, that is, whenever he moved his head too suddenly. His throat was parched, and he attributed that to the liquor. He recalled, too, that he had done some singing, and had an idea that that was probably equally responsible for his dryness. "Prairie Moon" rang in his ears. He remembered recruiting a quartet among the men at the bar. There was one fellow, a tall, pleasant fellow whose name Canavan couldn't remember; he'd insisted on buying Canavan a drink. Of course, not to be outdone, Canavan was certain that he had returned the compliment; now he wondered how many times he and his unknown friend had toasted each other. A sudden knock on the door jolted him back to reality. He turned quickly, made a wry face and put his hand to his head.

"Yeah?" he called.

The door opened, and a tall, smiling man appeared in the doorway.

"Mornin', Red," he said. "How d'you feel?"

Canavan thought he recognized the man. However, there was such a confused jumble of faces in his mind, he wasn't completely certain.

"Oh, awright," he replied.

The man closed the door behind him, leaned back against it and shoved his hat up from his eyes. He looked at Canavan again and smiled.

"Gotta hand it to you, partner. The way you lapped it up last night, I was sure you wouldn't be up an' around again f'r a week. You c'n handle your liquor awright, an' that's a heap more'n I c'n say 'bout a lot o' others in this town. Sa—ay, the way you're lookin' at me—don't you r'member me?"

Canavan sat down on the edge of the bed.

"Yeah, sure," he answered. "I had a drink with you last night, didn't I?"

"Y'mean one drink at a time. Alt'gether we must've had 'bout a dozen, or mebbe more."

"How'd I get in here?"

"Me an' Pete Collins lugged you up here and kinda dumped you into bed. You were pretty well talked out by then. You just rolled over an' went off t' sleep like a baby. What's the rest o' your name, Red?"

"Canavan."

"Don't s'ppose you r'member mine, do you?"

Canavan grinned sheepishly. "Nope," he admitted.

The man laughed softly. "Didn't expect you to. It's Quarles. My friends call me Dan," he said. He straightened up and sauntered across the room to the bed. "Look, Red, there's somethin' I wanna talk t' you about."

"Go ahead."

"We're votin' f'r sheriff t'night. I'd like t' have you vote f'r our man. How 'bout it?"

"Y'mean everybody's allowed t' vote, even strangers?"

"Long's you're here f'r twenty-four hours b'fore votin' time," Quarles replied.

"I see. Sure I'll vote f'r your man, Quarles."

"Dan."

"Dan," Canavan repeated. "What's his name?"

"Murray. Tex Murray. He's a swell feller, Red. You'll like 'im, too, same's everybody else does."

Canavan climbed to his feet. Quarles hitched up his belt.

"Thanks, Red," he said. He turned toward the door, halted again and looked back over his shoulder. "How 'bout droppin' in at Pete's place later on? 'Most everybody in town'll be there."

"Awright, mebbe I will. I'm gonna get me somethin' t' eat, and I know I c'n do with some fresh air. Then I'll come by."

Quarles nodded. "Swell," he said and went out.

An hour later Canavan rode slowly down the street. He spied Quarles and three other men idling in the open doorway of the "K. C." As he came abreast, Quarles looked up questioningly.

"Just gonna get me some air," Canavan called, and Quarles nodded understandingly. "See you soon."

He clattered out of town and swung on to a dirt road that wound southward over the range. The air was clear and crisp and he breathed it in deeply and hungrily. The grass was young and fresh and its fragrance filled the morning air. Logan fell away behind him. He heard the clatter of hoofs of an approaching horse and he twisted around in the saddle and looked back. A rider—it was a girl astride a white horse—topped a rise, spurred her mount and came whirling down the grassy incline. Canavan pulled up and waited. Presently the girl rode up to him. He touched his hat.

"Mornin'," he said.

The girl was pretty—he saw that at a glance—and he eyed her with youthful appreciation. It was only afterwards that he recalled that she hadn't acknowledged his greeting, but by then it didn't matter. She swung her horse around, ranging him alongside of Canavan's. He watched her, wonderingly and not too alertly, and as a result he was taken completely by surprise a moment later when the muzzle of a gun was jammed hard against his ribs.

"Don't try any tricks," she said coldly. "This gun shoots and I know how to shoot it."

"What's the idea?" he asked.

She did not answer. Instead she came closer to him and prodded him again with her gun. Her free arm slid around him, and his gun was jerked out of his holster. Then she backed her mount away.

"All right," she said. "We're riding south. Just remember what I told you about my gun."

They jogged away with Canavan riding slightly ahead of her. They rode in silence with nothing but the muffled thumping of their horses' hoofs to break the stillness of the morning air. They halted half an hour later atop a rise. Below them, stretching far southward, lay a fertile valley, rich with color.

"That trail below," the girl said, and Canavan followed her eyes. "Follow it and you'll be all right."

"I'm headin' f'r California," he answered quietly. "That's west, not south."

Their eyes met and clashed. The muzzle of her gun came up a bit higher until it gaped at his chest.

"Well?" she demanded coldly.

12

He shrugged his broad shoulders. "Reckon there ain't no argument against a Colt. You win."

He settled himself deeply in the saddle, turned slightly and looked at her again. His hand shot out suddenly, gripped her gun hand in a steely vise. Slowly the muzzle of her gun tilted, then it pointed skyward. Their faces were close together, a matter of inches between them. Their eyes met again, but neither spoke. Then he reached over with his free hand and took her gun. He sat back in the saddle.

"Awright," he said presently. "Let's have it. What's the idea o' tryin' to run me outa town?"

He spied the butt of his own gun peeking out at him from her wide leather belt. He grunted, leaned forward again and drew it out, shoving it down into his holster. Gravely he handed her her gun, butt first.

"Put it away," he said simply. He watched quietly as she returned it to her belt. "Well?"

Now she lowered her eyes, avoiding his.

"We didn't want you to vote tonight," she said in a small voice.

"I see. And you figgered the best way t' make sure I didn't vote was t' get rid o' me. Right?"

She did not answer.

"But why?" he demanded. "Don't tell me my one vote means so danged much that—"

"It means everything," she said, interrupting him.

He eyed her sharply.

"It does? How come?"

"There are three hundred and one voters in Logan," she explained without looking up. "Quarles controls one hundred and fifty of them. We can count on the others, one hundred and fifty-one. Of course one vote is the barest of margins, still that one vote means victory for us. Your vote would make it a tie, and with no legal curb on Quarles's gangs, they'd simply run wild."

"I see," he said again, thoughtfully. "But how d'you know I'm gonna vote f'r Quarles's man?"

"We kept tabs on you," she said quickly. "We know you spent last night in the 'K. C.,' drinking with Quarles, and that this morning he visited you in your room in the Standard Hotel."

"Oh," he said a bit lamely. "And who's your man?"

"John Richards."

"What makes him so much better'n that Murray feller?"

She raised her eyes to meet his.

"John Richards is a good man. He's honest and law-abiding. I know," she said simply, "because he's my father."

Canavan's eyebrows arched.

"Oh, so that's how it is!"

"Yes," she said, and now her eyes were unwavering. He caught himself admiring the fullness of her throat. "Logan was a peaceful little town till Quarles came. And because of him others like him came, too, until now they've almost taken the town over for themselves. We've got to keep them in check, or Logan will become a haven for the worst element the West has ever known. Then we'll be run out."

Canavan had listened attentively. Now he found himself nodding in agreement. He checked himself quickly.

"Your father know you're out campaignin' f'r him with a six gun?" he asked.

"No," she said and colored.

"Then you'd better make tracks f'r home pronto," he said, "b'fore someb'dy tells 'im."

"But—"

"Go on!" he said gruffly.

She wheeled her horse.

"Wait a minute," he said, and she pulled up and looked at him over her shoulder. "What's your name?"

"Beth."

"Beth," he repeated, grinning at her boyishly. "That's a nice name."

There was no response from her, no acknowledgment. He frowned and stiffened in the saddle.

"Go on!" he said brusquely. "Go on home where you b'long! And next time you'd better be careful who you go pullin' a gun on!"

She rode away slowly. He followed her with his eyes until she disappeared northward.

"If I sounded t' her like I did t' me," he muttered presently, "I'll bet I sure sounded like hell. I'm some tough hombre, awright. Bet she's gigglin' f'r all she's worth. What's more, I'll bet she knows doggoned well her ol' man's gonna win by two votes 'stead o' one!"

2. Blood on the Moon

It was election night in Logan, a clear, cool, starlit and moon-bright night with more activity on the town's street than anyone had ever witnessed there before. There were buckboards and farm wagons parked at various points along the street. There was even an old prairie schooner among them, and its huge, far-spread canvas top towered high above the other wagons. Passersby stopped and looked at it and grinned. There were gaps and rips in the canvas where it had simply rotted away. On the sides of the canvas were the words "California or Bust." A thick line of black paint had been drawn through the first two words, and the letters "ed" added to the remaining word, making it read "Busted."

From late afternoon through early evening the street had resounded with the echoing clatter of horses' hoofs. Contrary to expectations, Quarles's men had come early. They drifted into town unhurriedly, pulled up in front of the "K. C.," their usual meeting place, dismounted and tied up their horses, and sauntered inside for a drink or two. It was shortly after sundown when the first of the cattlemen rode into town. Each outfit loped into Logan in a compact body, headed by its owner and foreman. Some of the cattlemen—those who had brought their families along—came in the horse-drawn vehicles. There was no sign now of their women and children, evidence that they had been instructed to keep within the confines of their wagons.

From all indications it appeared that Quarles had ordered his men to keep to their side of the street. Now they were standing about idly, talking and laughing among themselves and occasionally stealing a glance across the street at the tight, silent little band of punchers and ranchers who leaned against darkened store fronts or shifted their weight from one leg to the other while they waited patiently for the voting to begin. They were quiet and grim-faced, for to them the matter of electing a sheriff was serious business.

Every now and then the tinkling of a piano's keys drifted streetward from the "K. C.," a voice was raised in song, then was drowned out by a roar of laughter. There was the screeching of a hand brake, and presently a farm wagon lumbered into town. Everyone looked up interestedly. The wagon rolled past the "K. C.," and a couple of men, appearing in the open doorway, followed it with their eyes until it braked again to a full stop far down the street. They watched for a moment as four men climbed out. As they turned away, the newcomers slung their rifles over their shoulders; then, in twos, they trudged up the street to fall in beside their waiting comrades from the ranches. There were, of course, the usual outbreaks among the tied-up horses. There were occasional tramplings and crowdings and constant millings about, and once a horse cried out in pain. Ironshod hoofs lashed out wildly, but somehow, strangely enough, the disturbance ended almost immediately.

Logan boasted of a bank and a newspaper publishing plant; it boasted of them because most towns of similar size had neither bank nor newspaper. The National Bank of Logan and the Logan *Bugle* occupied adjoining stores in the same building, a structure that stood about a hundred feet down the street from the "K. C." It was long past the bank's usual closing hour and its lights had long since been extinguished; there was a light in the *Bugle* office and two men idled in its open doorway eyeing the street scene. The tall, white-haired, dignified-looking man was Colonel Tom Wynn, the Kentucky-born owner of the bank. His companion was short and stocky and bald-headed, and the yellow lamplight behind him seemed to make his hairless head shine with unusual brightness. Everyone—that is, everyone save Colonel Wynn—called him or referred to him as Hank; the Colonel, of course, always called him Henry. The placard in the *Bugle* window read, "Henry Eustis Comerford, Jr., Publisher and Editor," and it had evidently left its imprint on Wynn's memory. Hank was a Virginian by birth but had lived most of his life in so many different States that he had acquired something of each State's speech and manner of speaking, and now it was such a full combination of dialects and inflections and gestures that it was impossible for anyone to tell with any degree of certainty just where Henry Comerford hailed from. Hank was just as undignified as the Colonel was dignified. He liked to laugh, and when he laughed he seemed to enjoy himself to the fullest. Wynn was thoughtfully silent. Hank looked up at him.

"What's botherin' you, Colonel?" he asked.

"Henry," Colonel Wynn answered heavily, "I've been

everywhere and I've always felt that I had seen everything, or practically everything."

"Well?"

"I'm sure I've never seen such a collection of low characters anywhere. Where in heaven's name did they all come from?"

"Y'mean Quarles's polecats?"

"Certainly."

"Dunno, Colonel," Comerford said. "But I've been lookin' 'em over and I recognize every last one o' th'm. Quarles hasn't rung in any outsiders. I expected 'im to and he's surprised me. They're his men, awright, and they're all entitled to a vote."

Wynn shook his head sadly.

"What a miscarriage of justice and the right of franchise!" he said, and he shook his head again. "In Kentucky we'd never have permitted such men to cast a vote."

"Dunno 'bout Kentucky," Hank said quickly. "In Virginia we'd never have let those polecats cross the State line!"

The Colonel frowned, gave him a sharp look but made no further comment.

"You ever been in Texas?" Hank asked.

"No."

"Well, all I wish right now is that we had a couple o' Texas Rangers here in Logan. What would happen then would really be somethin', believe me!"

"I've heard of the Texas Rangers' exploits."

Comerford snorted loudly. "Hearin' of 'em is one thing, but seein' 'em in action is somethin' else again. Doggone it, Colonel, you wouldn't have t' have more'n just a couple o' Rangers t' handle this gang. I r'member one time when I was in Laredo. That's in Texas, y' know."

"So I assumed," Wynn said dryly, "since you've been talking about the Texas Rangers."

Hank laughed softly. "We were talkin' about th'm at that, weren't we?"

Colonel Wynn looked at him and smiled. "Go on with your story, Henry," he said.

"We—ll," Hank began, "the way I r'member it, there was a killin' one night in one o' Laredo's toughest spots, a saloon run by 'n ornery cuss named O'Dea. There wasn't any sense in hollerin' f'r the sheriff 'cause everybody knew he was bedded down at the time with a busted

17

leg. Seems he'd taken part in a man hunt and stopped a couple o' slugs puttin' the quietus on some bad men who'd robbed a bank in a neighborin' town and who'd got the fool idea that they could make it to the border with the loot and their hides."

"Did they?"

"No, doggone it, they didn't! But since this ain't their story, that'll be all about them f'r now. Anyway, one o' Laredo's citizens got word o' the killin' to the Rangers at their Huntsville headquarters. They sent one man t' Laredo."

"One man, indeed!" the Colonel said, obviously impressed. "However, I assume that one man proved adequate; otherwise you wouldn't have chosen this story as an example of Ranger capability."

"Adequate?" Comerford echoed, bristling with indignation. "That, Colonel Wynn, is a gross understatement!"

The banker smiled. The newspaper publisher eyed him; then he smiled, too, in his tongue-in-cheek manner.

"I'm sorry, Henry. I hope both you and the Ranger in question will forgive me."

"We—ll," Hank said gravely, "long's you put it that way, reckon we c'n afford t' be big about it and let it pass. But to get back t' Laredo!"

"By all means, back to Laredo!"

"This Ranger feller," Hank continued, "he was a big feller, all right. I c'n almost picture 'im now, plain as if he was comin' down the street right now. He pulled up in front o' the saloon, when the owner, O'Dea, come out. O'Dea kinda got the idea that he was man enough t' stop the law fr'm its duty. They put on the grandest brawl I've ever seen, and b'lieve me, Colonel, I've seen some honeys. That Ranger just about took O'Dea apart! Then he r'peated the job on O'Dea's saloon, only on a bigger scale."

"I take it he got his man?"

Comerford chuckled delightedly. "You take it right! He got the killer and four others he recognized in the place as bein' on the Rangers' wanted list, and then he rode all five o' th'm outa town without anyone darin' t' raise a single finger against 'im. As f'r O'Dea, he was never the same after that beautiful wallopin' he c'llected. He found out there was a heck of a big difference b'tween sluggin' drunks who couldn't fight back and tacklin' someb'dy who must've been trained on wildcats. Anyway, Colonel, that's the Texas Rangers for you!"

The Colonel looked at his watch. "It's ten o'clock," he announced. "You'd better lock up, Henry. Time we were heading for the polls."

An empty store had been converted into a voting place. Swinging lamps that hung from the ceiling rafters furnished the light. A crude table had been placed in the very middle of the floor. Behind it were two chairs; one was occupied by a rancher, the other by a Quarles representative. Quarles himself, surrounded by half a dozen of his men, stood at the rear of the store. Others of his men were deployed along one wall facing an approximately equal number of punchers lined up along the opposite wall. They eyed one another hostilely, but confined their feelings toward one another to cold looks. A line of voters had already formed in the open doorway. Now it started to move inside. The first man, a tall, blond youth, his hat in his hand, halted in front of the table. The rancher drew a long sheet closer and picked up a pencil.

"Awright," he said briskly. "Your name?"

The puncher grinned boyishly. "Aw, c'mon, Boss," he drawled. "You oughta know it by now. I've been c'llectin' m' pay fr'm you f'r nigh unto five years now."

The rancher looked up. He frowned impatiently. The youth, recognizing the storm signals, coughed behind a big, freckled hand.

"Baxter," he said quickly. "Willie Baxter. I'm free, white and over twenty-one and I'm votin' f'r John Richards."

"Baxter," the rancher droned and made a pencil check in a column on the sheet in front of him. "Richards."

A check was made in still another column.

"Next!"

Baxter grinned, put on his hat and wheeled away. Another man stepped forward.

"Hill," he said clearly. "Dave Hill."

"Hill," the rancher repeated. "Dave Hill. Who you votin' for, Dave?"

"On'y decent man runnin', Boss. John Richards."

A murmur ran through the crowded store. Hill, his hand on his gun butt, stared coldly, scornfully, at Quarles. The latter smiled and the puncher turned slowly and moved away.

"Valdez," a swarthy man, third in line, said quietly. "Pedro Valdez."

"Valdez, Pedro. Votin' f'r Murray?"

"Si, señor," the man said quickly. "But of course Pedro votes for the *Señor* Murray. The *Señor* Murray is a great man. The *Señor* Quarles has told me so, and who is there to doubt the word of the *Señor* Quarles?"

"Next!"

The line moved steadily forward now with man after man stepping briskly to the table, calling out his name and announcing his candidate's name. Soon, too, the punchers lining the wall, then the men facing them, and finally Quarles and the group surrounding him voted. A handful of punchers remained, and so did a small group of their opponents. Quarles retired again to the rear. Colonel Wynn and Hank Comerford appeared, took their places in the line, patiently waited their turn, went through the formalities and cast their votes. The Colonel left immediately; Comerford lingered to watch the proceedings. A tall, heavy-set man with graying eyebrows and mustache strode in, glanced at some of the punchers idling near the door, nodded to them and went directly to the table.

"Richards," he said quietly, and all eyes were turned to him. "John Richards."

"Richards," the rancher at the table repeated. "John Richards. Votin' f'r y'self, John?"

"I am."

The second man at the table got to his feet and leaned forward a bit, watched as the pencil checks were made in their proper places, then sat down again. Richards, turning away, came face to face with a lean, bronzed man who smiled at him.

"Evenin', John," the man said. Richards did not answer; he pushed past the man and strode out. The latter watched him for a moment, then shrugged his shoulders and stepped up to the table.

"Murray," he said simply and waited, his thumbs hooked in his gun belt.

"First name?"

"Tex."

"Murray," the rancher droned. "Tex Murray. Votin' f'r y'self?"

"How'd Richards vote?"

"F'r 'imself."

Murray smiled coldly. "That so? Reckon then I'd better do somethin' f'r m'self. Put down a vote f'r me, will you, Stanton?"

The rancher nodded and made the necessary pencil

checks. Murray watched for a moment and finally turned away. Quarles strode forward now.

"Got all your side's votes in now?" he asked.

Stanton nodded. "Yep."

"Then s'ppose you tally 'em up."

"They're tallied up a'ready. Hundred an' fifty f'r Murray, hundred an' fifty-one f'r Richards. Reckon that's that."

Quarles laughed softly. "Like hell it is," he answered, wheeled and marched swiftly to the door. The punchers standing there moved away a bit. He halted in the open doorway. "Slim!"

There was a sudden rush of booted feet.

"Yeah?"

"Come in here an' do your stuff!"

Quarles stepped back and a tall, gangling youth appeared in the doorway.

"Go ahead!" Quarles commanded. He followed the youth to the table. "You c'n take his vote, Stanton. Give 'im your name, Slim."

Stanton frowned. "Where'd you dig him up, Quarles?"

The latter grinned amiably. "Didn't hafta do no diggin' f'r him," he replied with a mechanical nod toward Slim. "Fact o' the matter is, Stanton, Slim's been in Logan f'r more'n three days now. Nob'dy saw 'im when he got here 'cause it was durin' the night. Then I kept 'im under cover till sundown, when I turned 'im loose."

The frown on Stanton's face deepened.

"You cattlem'n ain't so all-fired smart," Quarles went on evenly. "Not by a jugful. Bet none o' you ever thought that mebbe a sucker like me could add same's you can an' that mebbe I knew all along how many votes you fellers had an' how many I could count on. So, while you an' the others were chucklin' up your sleeves an' takin' it f'r granted that th' 'lection was all over 'cept f'r the celebratin', I was out gettin' me 'n ace in the hole."

Stanton averted his eyes. He drew a deep breath and picked up his pencil stub again.

"What's your name?" he growled.

"Bennett," Slim replied. "Slim Bennett."

Stanton scribbled Bennett's name at the bottom of the sheet in front of him, then made a check mark alongside it. The man sitting beside him grinned. He looked up, caught Quarles's eye and winked.

"Votin' f'r Murray?" Stanton demanded.

Quarles laughed scornfully. "What d'you think?" he countered.

21

Stanton did not answer. He made a second check mark, this time in the column headed "Murray." Then he looked up.

"Well," he said to Quarles, "We're all even. Now what?"

"Even f'r now, you mean," Quarles said. "Just you hang on t' that pencil, mister. I ain't finished yet."

"What d'you mean?"

"Keep your shirt on," Quarles answered. He wheeled and strode to the door again. He cupped his hands around his mouth. "Canavan!"

There was a curious silence outside. It lasted but a brief minute, then a tall figure filled the doorway.

"Come in, Red," Quarles said. He turned quickly. "Here y'are, Stanton. Here's another name f'r you t' add t' that list. Red Canavan."

Canavan stepped forward to the table. Quarles followed at his heels. Stanton looked from one to the other.

"Well?" Quarles demanded.

Stanton's lips tightened. He wrote "Canavan" below Slim Bennett's name.

"Check off another vote f'r Murray," Quarles commanded impatiently.

"He's s'posed t'say **wh**o he's votin' f'r," Stanton grumbled, "not you."

Quarles laughed again. "Oh, yeah? Speak your piece, Red."

"I'm votin' f'r John Richards," Canavan said quietly.

For a moment no one moved. There was no sound save the heavy breathing of the men watching the little drama at the table. Stanton stared at Canavan incredulously.

"R—Richards?" he repeated hollowly.

"That's what he said," Quarles said. He laughed again and clapped Canavan on the back. "That's awright, Red. This is a free country an' you c'n vote f'r anybody you like."

Stanton excitedly made a double check mark opposite Canavan's name, laughed and tossed his pencil stub in the air. He pushed his chair back, when somewhere along the street a rifle cracked with a curiously spiteful whine. Stanton froze, his hands on the edge of the table. Every man in the place stiffened. Then a woman's scream echoed the length of the street. There was a shuffling of booted feet. A man moved, and there was a sudden headlong rush for the door. The street was filled with running men.

"It's Richards!" a man yelled over his shoulder as he raced past the crowded doorway. "He's layin' sprawled out on his face!"

3. Canavan Hires Out ★

IT WAS three days after John Richards's death, two days after his funeral—long, tense, nerve-racking days with both sides maintaining a grim and forbidding silence, and with each side needing but a single hostile move on the part of the other to indulge itself in an outpouring of its pent-up feelings toward the other. Richards's sudden and untimely death had left a tremendous gap in the cattlemen's ranks, for admittedly he had been the strongest man among them; now they seemed hesitant, even lost, without acknowledged leadership. True, they made no attempt to return to their homes, but lingered on in Logan with a curious doggedness, eyeing Quarles's men across the street as though they hoped one of them would do something to touch off the emotional powder keg. But Quarles's grip on his followers was secure and absolutely unyielding. His men kept their distance and refrained from further antagonizing the cattlemen, most of whom had insisted at the very moment of Richards's killing that the lawless element be wiped out. They saw no reason for waiting; they wanted vengeance and they wanted it without delay.

Of course older and self-admittedly wiser heads among them cautioned against such a rash idea; they needed numerical superiority over Quarles before they would agree to attack him. They warned the younger and hotter heads that if they abandoned reason and plunged blindly into an attack, the result would be the worst blood-letting the West had ever known. The younger men gave in after a while, but insisted on having the last word in the argument. They demanded and received the older men's promise that if Quarles's men committed a single offense against them, there would be a general attack on them.

Now, it was three days later and half a dozen of the most influential ranchers had come together in the very store in which they and their punchers had elected John Richards to the office of sheriff. Burly Ed Hockett had asked for the meeting. Now he faced them, his big hands on his ample hips. White-haired Matt Fox and bald-headed Larry Parker, lean Will Davis and blond Charlie Baldwin, leaned back against one wall; on the opposite side of the store, the Gillen twins, Les and Jerry, the youngest of the ranchers, waited patiently for big Ed to speak. Hockett finally shoved his hat up from his eyes.

"Men," he began, "I've been doin' a lotta thinkin' 'bout things an' I've come t' one c'nclusion. Just b'tween you, me an' that spider up there in that ceilin' beam, Quarles's got us stopped. What's worse, he knows it an', bein' cute, he's just sittin' tight an' lettin' us knock ourselves out figgerin' an' plannin' an' gettin' nowheres fast. We got just one way o' fixin' Mister Quarles an' that is by outsmartin' 'im."

The ranchers nodded mutely.

"Awright then," Hockett continued. "I've got 'n idea, but b'fore I spill it, I want you fellers t' promise me that you'll keep your mouths shut f'r two hull minutes after I've finished. Then, after you've had two minutes' time t' think over what I've said, if any o' you don't cotton t' my idea, you just say so an' I'll f'rget th' hull thing. That a deal?"

There was a general nodding of heads. Jerry Gillen made it even more emphatic by adding aloud: "Sure, Ed. What've we got t' lose by hearin' you out?"

"Thanks," big Ed said dryly. "I'm s'ggestin' that we appoint Beth Richards t' the job her father was 'lected to an' dare Quarles t' do somethin' about it."

Jerry Gillen whistled softly. His brother glared at him, and Jerry averted his eyes hastily.

"I ain't finished yet," Hockett said presently. "Lemme tell you fellers what's b'hind my idea. First, if we go after Quarles, it'll be a stand-off. He's got th' same number o' men that we've got. We'll kill his men off an' they'll kill ours. It don't make sense t' me an' I hope t' hell it don't t' you fellers. Wa—al, s'ppose we act smart, too, an' use some sense. You know well's I do, if we give Beth th' job, he won't open 'is mouth. He won't dare to. Awright then. Actu'lly she'll on'y be a front f'r us. We'll be able t' take wallops at Quarles an' he won't be able t' hit back 'cause we'll be doin' it on th' side o' th' law. Get it? Then, too, if we're smart, while we're whittlin' down Quarles's gang, we c'n be addin' men t' our outfits, an' when we figger we're able to take on th' job like we're gonna hafta do some day, we'll really go after Quarles an' finish him off. That's th' story, an' now you fellers have got two minutes t' think it over."

Hockett turned away from the table. He walked unhurriedly to the door, opened it and, halting in the doorway, looked out into the street. Mother Jones appeared in her doorway and eyed him. Big Ed grunted, backed inside and slammed the door shut.

"Ed," Matt Fox called, and Hockett turned around.

"Yeah?"

"How d'you know Beth'll take th' job?"

"I've a'ready sounded 'er out an' she's willin'."

Fox shrugged his shoulders.

"I'm f'r th' idea," he said. "Leastways, th' way I see it, let's give it a try, an' then, if it don't work, we'll call it off."

Hockett nodded.

"Thanks, Matt," he said. "I was kinda countin' on you t' be willin' t' try it. Now how 'bout you other fellers? How 'bout it, Larry?"

"Oh, reckon I'll go along on it with you an' Matt," Parker responded. "Like Jerry said b'fore, what've we got t' lose by givin' it a try?"

"How 'bout you, Will?"

"You c'n count me in," Davis replied.

"Charlie?" Hockett asked, turning to Baldwin.

The latter nodded.

"Jerry? Les?"

"We'll play along with it, too," Les said.

"Swell."

"Looks like you've got everybody's vote, Ed," Matt Fox said. "Now who's gonna break it t' Quarles?"

"I am," Ed answered. "I've a'ready sent f'r him. He oughta be here 'most any minute now."

Matt grinned at him.

"Figgered we'd back you up all along, eh?"

"Yep," Hockett answered. "Feller oughta know who his friends are, oughtn't he, an' who he c'n count on?"

There was a loud rap on the door.

"There he is," Ed said and turned. "Come in!"

The door opened. Quarles, his thumbs hooked in his gun belt, stood in the doorway.

"Understan' you want t' see me, Hockett. That right?"

"Yeah. Come in, will yuh?"

"Awright."

Quarles stepped inside. He closed the door behind him with a backward thrust of his right leg. His eyes ranged over the other ranchers for a moment, then he looked at Hockett again. "What'd you want t' see me about?"

"Quarles," Ed began. He cleared his throat and went on again, "Quarles, we've picked us a sheriff."

"That so?"

"Yep, an' we figgered we oughta be the ones t' tell it to you 'stead o' havin' you get it fr'm someb'dy else."

"I'm listenin'."

"We've picked Beth Richards f'r the job," Hockett concluded.

Quarles concealed his surprise well. There was no change in his expression.

"You don't say!"

Big Ed grinned.

"Yeah," he said casually. "I s'ppose namin' a woman f'r sheriff is kinda outa th' ord'nary. Still, there ain't no reason why she shouldn't do awright f'r 'erself. F'r one thing, it's a pretty safe bet that she'll outlive a heap o' others we mighta picked. After all, pluggin' a man is one thing, but when it comes t' pluggin' a woman, hell, that's somethin' else again. It just ain't bein' done."

"What's that s'pposed t' mean?"

"Nuthin."

Quarles's lips tightened.

"That all you wanted t' see me about?" he asked.

Hockett nodded mutely. Quarles's eyes shifted; he looked at the Gillens, at Matt Fox and the others, sharply, grimly. Then he wheeled suddenly and stalked out. He halted briefly outside, flung a backward glance over his shoulder, jerked the door to him viciously; it slammed and he was gone. Ed turned to his companions and grinned.

"Reckon that's that," he said. "Fr'm the look on Mister Quarles's face, I'd say we just about kicked his plans right smack in the pants. Yep, I got 'n idea he's madder'n a wet hen right now, an' what I like about it is that he knows we've put a honey over on 'im an' he can't do a doggoned thing about it!"

Henry Comerford looked up from his desk to find a tall, lean, redheaded young man standing in front of him and watching him patiently.

"Howdy," Canavan said.

"Huh? Oh, h'llo! 'Fraid I didn't hear you come in. Something I c'n do f'r you?"

"That d'pends. That letterin' outside on the window reads 'Henry Eustis Comerford, Jr.' That you?"

"In the flesh, my friend."

"Where d'you come fr'm?"

"Virginia. To be more exact, Fairfax County."

"Uh-huh. Ever hear tell uva feller named Short?"

Comerford grinned broadly.

26

"And how!"

"What was 'is first name?"

"Luke," Comerford answered promptly. "He had two brothers, Tom and Ira. They were definitely the marryingest men I ever heard of. Tom and Ira had been married three times each when I saw them last. As for Luke—"

"He's even with th'm. Got married again just b'fore I left."

"You don't say!"

"Yep, he got hitched to a widow this time. Luke told me all about you an' said that if I ever ran across you, I was t' stop by an' say 'h'llo' f'r him. I've been on th' lookout f'r you f'r more'n eight months now. Seems like every town I hit, you've been there, awright—an' gone."

Comerford laughed sheepishly.

"That's right," he admitted. "In some places I just about get unpacked when I have to pack up again and get moving on. I don't seem to get along very well with certain elements when I start to take an interest in town politics."

"Y'mean you get run out?"

"Practically. However, usually I'm able to leave under my own power. You see, my friend, at the very outset I manage to make friends with some citizen who knows what is going on and through him I generally get an advance warning when things are about to happen to me. When I get the word, I simply throw my equipment together and off I go again. Of course it's a hectic life, still it has its good points."

"Yeah, I c'n see that. No chance o' you ever gettin' in a rut, eh?"

"Hardly."

"What's goin' on in this town?" Canavan asked.

"Oh, just a struggle between the law-abiding and the lawless," Comerford replied.

"Who d'you figger plugged Richards?"

"Who actually fired the fatal shot, I don't know. But there can't be any question as to who ordered it fired."

Canavan nodded understandingly.

"Wa—al, Mister, reckon I'll be goin' along now. I'll come by again sometime," he said.

"Do that," Comerford answered.

Canavan turned, hitched up his belt and went out. A minute later Colonel Wynn came striding in. There was a smile on Henry Comerford's face. The Colonel eyed him questioningly.

"Henry," he said.

"Huh? Oh, h'llo, Colonel!"

"You seem to be quite pleased about something."

Comerford laughed.

"I am, Colonel!" he replied. "Y'know, I think I'm going to like Logan after all. Why, I wouldn't be surprised if I even decided to settle down here and call it 'home.'"

Wynn smiled patiently.

"That's very interesting, Henry," he said. "I'm delighted to hear you talk that way. But what brought about your change of heart?"

Comerford laughed again, took him by the arm and led him to the open door.

"See that tall young feller going up the street?" he asked, nodding in the direction of the striding Canavan.

"Young fellow?" the Colonel repeated. "Oh, yes! I see him!"

"That's why I know Logan's going to be all right."

"I—I don't understand."

"You will, Colonel, you will."

"But who is that young fellow?" Wynn asked. "What's his name?"

"I don't know."

"I must say, Henry—"

"He's a Texan," Comerford interrupted. "He stopped in t' say 'hello' for Luke Short."

"Luke—Short?"

"Yes," Comerford went on. "I've told you about him before but you've probably forgotten his name. Luke is head o' the Texas Rangers."

"Oh, I see! And you think that man—the fellow going up the street—is a Ranger, too. Is that it?"

"Uh-huh. Even though he didn't say so, I've got 'n idea he's one o' them, all right!"

"Well, you talked with him, didn't you? Then why didn't you ask him?"

"You don't ask a question like that, Colonel!"

"Did he ask you any questions?"

"He wanted to know what was going on in this town."

"That might mean something," Colonel Wynn admitted.

"Of course it does! And so does the fact that Luke Short gave him a message for me. Now I'm waiting to see him do just one thing. If he goes into the sheriff's office, that should mean everything. I've noticed that whenever a Ranger comes into a town, the very first thing he does is head for the sheriff's office. Let's see if our young friend does!"

Canavan halted in front of a small store over whose doorway hung a sign that read "Sheriff." The door was closed, but through its glass panel he could see a girl standing beside a desk in the middle of the floor. He turned the knob, and the door opened. Beth Richards looked up. She looked tired and he saw at once that she was tight-lipped. Canavan took off his hat.

"Awright f'r me t' come in?" he asked.

"Of course," Beth answered.

Canavan stepped inside, closed the door and came forward.

"Wanted t' tell you how sorry I am 'bout what happened t' your father," he began. "I've been wonderin' 'bout it an' thinkin' that maybe if I hadn't o' voted for 'im, that maybe—"

"It wouldn't have made any difference," she interrupted, "that is, as far as his death is concerned. Your vote helped him win and I'm very grateful to you. But Quarles would have gotten Dad anyway, sometime or other, even if Dad hadn't won the election. He knew that Dad was the leader of the cattlemen, and he simply had to get him out of the way. So you mustn't feel responsible in the slightest."

"Wa—al, long's you say so, reckon it's awright then."

"It is," she insisted.

His eyes ranged over the store. There were half a dozen odd chairs in addition to the desk, but there were no other furnishings. He looked at her again.

"Think you're gonna like this job?" he asked.

"I'm sure I will if for no other reason than that it will give me an opportunity to avenge Dad's murder."

"Uh-huh. What about your deputies? Got 'em picked out a'ready?"

"I hope to have one deputy," she answered, "that is, if there's some way of raising enough money to pay a deputy's salary."

"I see. An' you got him picked out?"

"Frankly, no."

"Reckon, then, I'm in luck. I'm lookin' f'r a job."

She smiled fleetingly.

"A deputy sheriff's job doesn't pay very much," she explained.

"Oh, that's awright! Fact o' the matter is, I'd even take a deputy's job f'r no pay."

She eyed him curiously, wonderingly.

"Do I get it?" he asked with a grin.

"Yes, certainly," she said quickly. "But why do you want it?"

He shrugged his broad shoulders.

"Oh, I dunno. Mebbe it's just that I've never worked f'r a woman b'fore an' I wanna see what it's like," he replied casually.

Colonel Wynn and Henry Comerford were still standing in the *Bugle* doorway when Canavan came striding back. The publisher and Canavan nodded to each other. When he had passed, Comerford turned excitedly to the Colonel.

"Did you see it?" he demanded.

"See what?"

"The silver star on his shirt front," Comerford explained breathlessly. "He's a lawman, just as I figured he was! Now you just watch and see if Logan 'specially Quarles, doesn't roll over and play dead!"

4. Quarles Strikes Back ★

THE WEEK that followed was a quiet one, with nothing to mar Beth Richards's first taste of law enforcement. From the doorway of the sheriff's office they saw Quarles pass daily, saw his men come and go. Quarles never glanced across the street; his men clattered past and looked back sometimes over their shoulders, but that was as far as their hostility toward the law went. At night, of course, the "K. C." was, as usual, alive with trade; there too, however, laughter and song and loud voices never reached the troublesome stage. Canavan eyed the situation quietly and, whatever his thoughts were, he kept them to himself. While Beth was in town, he never left her alone; when she went down the street, he was always at her heels. Townsmen eyed the pair, the pretty girl and the tall, lean redhead with the big Colt swinging low against his right thigh, but nobody said anything; there was an all-too-apparent look of capability about Canavan that everyone seemed to recognize instantly. Then, too, there was a steely, ominous glint in Canavan's eyes whenever anyone's glance in Beth's direction lingered too long, and the offender, when he found the tall youth watching him, quickly flushed and turned away.

Beth came striding down the street one day. She looked back over her shoulder, gave Canavan a rebuking stare and halted, hands on hips, directly in his path.

"Johnny Canavan," she said severely and frowned.

"Huh?" he said and halted too.

"Will you please stop following me around?"

"Heck," he said with his boyish grin, "c'n I help it if I'm allus runnin' into you wherever I go?"

She realized how futile it was to say any more, turned without another word and went on. She stole another backward look over her shoulder, and Canavan was right behind her, an expression of complete innocence on his face. She turned a corner and collided with a man who muttered something under his breath, then reached out to grab her arm, when Canavan stepped directly in front of him. Both men looked at each other. Neither said a word, but presently it was the second man who averted his eyes, turned and trudged off. Beth offered no objections, after that experience, to Canavan's dogging her.

Canavan kept his room at the Standard. It was handy to the office, and his closeness to it provided him with the excuse he always offered for being there, ready and waiting, when Beth arrived in the morning. In the evening it was he who locked up, helped her mount and rode part of the way home with her. A couple of miles out of town they halted. Canavan wheeled his horse.

"Wa—al," he said lightly, "take care o' yourself, Boss, an' I'll see you in th' mornin'."

"Johnny," she said.

"Yeah?"

"I'm moving into town tomorrow."

He eyed her for a moment.

"Y'are? Why?"

"I think I ought to be closer to the office than I am. I should be the one to open the office and close it, not you. As it is, you do everything, or whatever there is to do, and in return you get absolutely nothing. It's—it's the most ridiculous arrangement I ever heard of."

He grinned at her.

"Mebbe. But t' me it's th' doggonedest swellest job I ever had. So long's I ain't beefin' 'bout things, why should you, huh? G'wan, you better get goin' b'fore it gets dark."

"You're a stubborn mule, Johnny Canavan."

"Yeah, reckon that's so, Beth, an' since we both know it an' realize we can't do a danged thing about it, why don't we just f'rget it, huh?"

She looked at him for a moment. He grinned at her again and she shook her head.

"I give up," she said finally.

"Now you're talkin' sense. G'night, Beth."

She settled herself in the saddle.

"Good night, Johnny," she said and loped off.

"Hey!" he called and she reined in, twisted around and looked back. "You f'rget that business 'bout movin' into town, y'hear?"

She spurred her mount and sent him whirling away.

It was about ten o'clock that night and Canavan was lounging in the doorway of the office when Quarles emerged from the "K. C." Canavan, watching him interestedly, saw him saunter up the street aimlessly. Presently Quarles came abreast of him, looked over at him for a moment and finally crossed the street.

"H'llo, Red."

"Oh, h'llo, Quarles."

"How's th' job comin' along?"

"Awright."

There was a sudden echoing clatter of hoofs and both men turned. A handful of men appeared in the doorway of the "K. C." and peered out. A horseman came thundering into town, flashed past the "K. C.," swerved and pulled up in front of the office. Canavan straightened up. The horseman swung himself out of the saddle and strode straight to the doorway.

"S'matter?" Canavan asked.

"Better get your horse, Mister," the man panted. "We've been—"

"Wa—al?" Canavan demanded.

The man looked sharply at Quarles. Without another word he pushed past Canavan into the office. Canavan followed at his heels and kicked the door shut behind him.

"You wanna watch your step, Mister," the man said. "That feller's bad medicine. You oughta know that."

"You stick t' your knittin', partner," Canavan said sharply. "I'll stick t' mine, an' I'll take care o' mine. Now what's all th' excitement about?"

The man frowned.

"Suit y'self," he said gruffly. "We've been raided an' some o' our cattle run off."

"What's your outfit?"

"Th' Bar-X. Matt Fox is my boss."

"Awright. You wait out front f'r me till I get my horse. I won't be more'n a minute."

Two minutes later they rode swiftly out of town and dashed into the night-darkened range. Logan disappeared behind them, and when Canavan twisted around, and looked back, there was no sign of it. Settling himself in the saddle, he let the Bar-X man take the lead, holding his own well-rested mount in check despite the latter's efforts to get his head and run freely. They rode steadily eastward, with the thick range grass muffling the rhythmic pounding of their horses' hoofs. Presently Canavan relaxed his grip on the reins and his mount bounded forward. When they came alongside the puncher's horse, Canavan turned his head.

"Pull up!" he called and both horses slid to a stop.

The puncher looked at Canavan quickly.

"S'matter?" he asked. "Your horse go lame?"

"Nope. Just got 'n idea an' I figger I'd better ask you a couple o' questions."

"Can't they wait till we get t' th' ranch?" the man countered. "Seems t' me, Mister—"

"Never mind what it seems like t' you," Canavan said sharply, interrupting him. "I ain't goin' out t' th' Bar-X just yet. Th' raiders ain't there. They've hitailed it. I aim t' follow th'm."

"Oh!"

"How many o' th'm were there?"

"Oh, 'bout ten."

"Uh-huh. How many head they get away with?"

"B'tween two hundred an' two hundred an' fifty."

"Which way'd th' raiders go afterwards?"

"North."

"Hill country up there?"

"An' how!"

"You fellers follow th'm?"

"Wa—al," the puncher answered a bit lamely, "we didn't go after 'em soon's we shoulda. Y'see, Mister, there were on'y two o' th' boys ridin' herd. We didn't figger we needed more'n two f'r a job like that. Anyway, it seems like th' raiders swooped down on th'm all uva sudden-like."

"Yeah," Canavan said dryly. "Raiders allus seem t' bust in on things kinda sudden-like. 'Bout time someb'dy wised 'em up t' th' fact that it ain't th' right thing t' do, 'specially at night when a feller's eyes don't want t' stay open an' 'is backside wishes it was outa th' saddle an' parked in a bunk."

The Bar-X man did not answer.

"You were talkin' 'bout havin' on'y two fellers ridin' herd," Canavan said.

"Oh, yeah! Wa—al, Bob Mack was ridin' roun' th' herd. Bob's partner, Petey Dixon, had gone off t' th' line shack t' get somethin'. He heard the shootin'—"

"What shootin'?"

"Th' raiders spotted Bob an' opened up on 'im."

"Oh!"

"Bob caught a slug in 'is shoulder an' toppled outa th' saddle. Fr'm then on, things happened so fast that by th' time Petey come gallopin' back, it was all over. Th' raiders were gone an' so was th' herd. Petey sized things up an' figgered th' thing f'r him t' do was t' get Bob back t' th' house an' then rouse us. But by th' time we got th' other boys routed outa their bunks an' into th' saddle, it was too late. Th' boys went off fin'lly, but they couldn't find a doggoned thing. They circled aroun' an' aroun', but in th' dark it was no go. They gave up after a while an' hotfooted it back t' th' house."

"I see."

"Th' boss d'cided it was a job f'r th' law an' sent me off t' town," the man concluded.

"Two hundred an' fifty head o' cattle ain't enough t' hold up a bunch o' raiders f'r long," Canavan mused aloud. "Not if th' raiders know their business. They coulda moved pretty fast, y'know."

" 'Course."

"Look, partner," Canavan said shortly. "You go on t' your place. You tell your boss I'll be there t' see him later on. I know where th' Bar-X spread is. Beth Richards told me."

"Awright."

The man spurred his mount and dashed away. Canavan wheeled his horse and rode northward into the silent night.

It was dawn when Canavan halted his mount atop a rise that looked down upon a saucer-like valley below. He shifted himself stiffly in the saddle and kicked his feet free of the stirrups.

"Reckon that's it," he muttered wearily. "An' 'less I miss my guess, Matt Fox is gonna raise hell when I tell 'im I didn't find hide nor hair o' his herd. Beth told me he's hell-on-wheels when he gets riled. I'm so doggoned tired it won't take a heap o' hollerin' at me t' get me riled up, so Mister Fox an' me oughta do awright t'gether."

He could see a low, sprawling ranch house. Its fresh white paint gleamed with unusual brightness despite the drab light of approaching day. There was a huge barn, with the doors open, beyond the house itself, a lean-to with a blacksmith's anvil, and, to the left of the barn, a corral with half a dozen horses idling about within the barred enclosure. There was also a low, squat building to complete the ranch scene, and Canavan recognized it as the usual ranch type of bunkhouse. In the doorway were two men armed with rifles. Canavan's booted feet nosed into the stirrups; he tightened his grip on the reins, wheeled his horse and guided him down a winding trail. The animal's iron shoes clattered sharply over a stretch of stony ground. Presently they reached the base of the trail, and when Canavan looked up he saw the men in the bunkhouse doorway and another group just beyond the structure staring in his direction. He nudged his horse with his knees and they went forward toward the corral at a canter. A man dashed around the corral, halted and cupped his hands around his mouth.

"Matt!" he hollered.

Canavan grinned broadly. He nodded to the man when he came abreast of him, then clattered past the corral. The door in the white house opened and a white-haired man appeared. He stepped outside and a girl in a red blouse and dungarees followed at his heels. Both stopped short and looked at Canavan. He clattered up to them, reined in, eyed the girl appreciatively and nodded to the man at her side.

"Mornin'," he said gravely. "I'm Canavan. Reckon you must be Matt Fox. Right?"

The rancher nodded.

"You find anything?" he asked.

Canavan eased himself in the saddle and pushed his dust-flecked hat up from his eyes.

"Nope."

A frown darkened Fox's face.

"That's fine," he said gruffly. "Two hundred an' forty-one head o' cattle gone plumb t' hell an' no sign o' th' way they went. Y'know, Mister, if you'da used s'me sense an' come straight out here 'stead o' goin' off by y'self an' wastin' a lotta valu'ble time, some o' my boys coulda gone 'long with you an' showed you the way t' th' Pass, 'cause, sure as shootin', that's where my cattle went."

"They didn't go through th' Pass," Canavan said quietly.

The rancher's eyes gleamed angrily.

"How'n hell d'you know?" he demanded.

"I know," Canavan said calmly, " 'cause I rode through

th' Pass an' there wasn't a single split hoof track inside th' Pass or outside uv it."

Fox's lip curled scornfully.

"Sure," he said curtly, "th' earth just opened an' swallowed 'em up."

"Mebbe," Canavan replied. "On'y I don't think so. You got any other ideas or s'ggestions I c'n work on?"

"You're s'pposed t' be th' lawm'n 'round here," Fox snapped, "not me. It's your job t' find them cattle. Go figger out f'r y'self what coulda happened to 'em. Now s'ppose you get outa here an' get busy 'stead o' sittin' up there an' givin' me a lotta sass!"

Canavan's lips tightened into a thin line.

"S'ppose you go t' hell!" he said coldly.

"Why, you—!" Fox yelled. He jerked his right arm backward, clumsily, yanked out his gun and snapped it upward. "Now, you young polecat—!"

"Yeah?" Canavan taunted him.

"You get th' hell offa my place an' stay off it!" Fox roared. "What's more, if you don't find out what happened t' my cattle, I'll run you outa Logan so fast nob'dy'll see you f'r dust!"

Four men with rifles in their hands sauntered up and ranged themselves behind their irate employer. Canavan eyed them briefly, then shifted his attention back to Fox.

"Go on!" the rancher commanded. "Get goin' b'fore I lose m' temper an' start shootin'!"

"I'm goin'," Canavan said calmly, "but it ain't on account o' that gun you're wavin' around. If you can't shoot any better'n you c'n pull a gun, you oughta go put it away b'fore it goes off an' scares th' pants offa you. If I'da wanted to, I coulda blasted you t' hell'n gone b'fore you got your gun outa th' holster, b'lieve me, Mister."

One of the punchers, a heavy-set, round-shouldered man, pushed forward now.

"Awright," he said gruffly. "We've heard enough outa you. Get goin'!"

He reached for Canavan's bridle. The redheaded youth's booted foot swung upward. There was a dull, muffled crack, and the puncher cried out and staggered away, clutching at his injured arm. Canavan wheeled his horse and jogged off. He heard a shout behind him but disregarded it. When he reached the corral gate, a couple of men came sprinting toward him from the bunkhouse and he pulled up and waited. They panted to a stop in front of him.

"Get down offa there!" one man ordered.

Canavan grinned coldly, dangerously.

"Mebbe you'd like t' try an' make me," he answered. His right hand dropped to the butt of his gun. There was no movement among the men. "S'matter, flannel mouth? Lose your nerve? Reckon all you Bar-X'ers—an' that goes double f'r your boss—talk too damned much an' do too damned little. Go on, get outa my way."

Fox's punchers glared at him.

"Wa—al?" he demanded roughly.

When there was no movement among the men in front of him, he jerked out his gun in a lightning draw. The cattlemen moved quickly then and backed out of his way. He grunted contemptuously, holstered his gun and rode off again. When he came to the base of the winding trail, he twisted around and looked back for a moment. Then he sent his horse up the grass and stone path that led the level of the range.

5. Double Trouble ★

BETH was troubled. Her eyes probed Canavan's earnest face.

"I tell you, Beth, there's somethin' doggoned rotten 'round these parts," Canavan said for the second time. "F'r my money, it's so rotten it smells out loud."

"But, Johnny," she said finally, "I don't seem to understand. Just what do you think really happened to those Bar-X steers? Suppose your theory is correct and they never reached the Pass. Then where did they go?"

Canavan leaned forward over the desk.

"Wanna know what I really think? I got 'n idea th' raiders simply swung 'em eastward aroun' th' Bar-X," he answered.

"Eastward?" she repeated.

"Uh-huh. Get th' idea?"

"Y—es, but then what?"

"There's either some hidin' place they got f'r holin' up rustled cattle," he continued, "or else some rancher is dealin' 'em off th' bottom."

"What—what do you mean?"

"I mean that one o' th' ranchers is playin' both ends against th' middle."

"Johnny, I still don't understand."

"What I'm tryin' t' tell you, Beth, without sayin' it right out, is that one o' th' ranchers is workin' with th' other ranchers an' with Quarles, both at th' same time. That clear now?"

"O—h!"

"Figger it out f'r y'self," Canavan went on. "Two hundred an' forty-one head o' cattle don't just up an' disappear into thin air. Th' raiders musta had a place t' hide 'em away b'fore they hit th' Bar-X, an' f'r my dough they proved it by simply whiskin' th' herd clear offa th' range without leavin' a single track b'hind th'm. I know it sounds r'diculous, but I'm willin' t' bet every buck I'll ever have that that's what happened to 'em."

"You didn't mention that idea to Fox, did you?"

Canavan straightened up.

"To that flea-bitten ol' coot? Nope."

He shifted his holster to his hip.

"Beth, there's another idea I've been toyin' with. Mebbe it's even more r'diculous than th' first one."

She looked up quickly.

"I got t' wonderin', when I couldn't find any trace o' th' missin' cattle, that mebbe th' Bar-X wasn't raided at all."

"You mean that Fox—?"

"Cooked up th' hull thing."

"I can't believe that, Johnny. Matt Fox—well, if you knew him as I do and as Dad did, you'd know he couldn't do such a thing. I admit he has a violent temper and a terrible tongue, but he's honest, Johnny. You must be wrong!"

Canavan shrugged his shoulders.

"Till I know f'r sure that Mister Fox ain't doin' some fancy double-dealin'," he said doggedly, "I'm puttin' him down in my book on th' same page with Quarles."

"If I were a man," they heard a voice say. They turned quickly. Matt Fox's daughter stood in the doorway, her hand on the doorknob. Her eyes gleamed with the same anger that Canavan had seen in her father's eyes. "If I were a man," she repeated coldly, "I'd kill you for coupling my father's name with Quarles's!"

Beth got to her feet.

"Peggy—"

The girl came forward to the desk. Canavan moved away. He leaned back against the wall. Peggy, turning her back on him, faced Beth.

"I came to tell you that there was another raid early this morning," she said briefly.

38

Beth gasped aloud, and Canavan's head jerked up.

"It was the Bar-O this time," Peggy continued. "One of their line-riders, old Danny Hart, brought us word of it. He'd been shot, and he barely managed to make it to our place and tell us what had happened before he died."

"The Bar-O," Canavan heard Beth say, "Ed Hockett's outfit."

"Yes," Peggy said, then turned on her heel and went swiftly to the door. She turned in the doorway for a parting shot. "Now, Mister Deputy, if there's still room on that page in your book, you'd better add Ed Hockett's name to your growing list of suspects. Since he too has been victimized, that makes him a suspect along with my father, doesn't it?"

Peggy stormed out, slamming the door behind her. Canavan, his jaw muscles twitching, turned slowly. His thumbs hooked in his gun belt, he walked to the window and peered out into the street. He looked up when a man astride a big white horse jogged by. It was Quarles, and he glanced at the tight-lipped man in the window and nodded to him.

"One o' these fine days," Beth heard Canavan say through his teeth, "I'm gonna tangle with that polecat. An' when I do, I'm gonna kill him, or he's gonna hafta kill me. It'll hafta be like that 'cause this town ain't big enough f'r both uv us an' I don't aim t' leave it 'less I'm carried out!"

He came away from the window and strode back to the desk. She looked up at him quietly.

"I'm goin' out t' Hockett's place," he said with finality. "Mebbe I c'n do s'me good out there. But you're stayin' put. An' if I ain't back by sundown, don't you go frettin' none, understand? It'll just be that I'm workin' on somethin' that I can't quit."

Beth nodded mutely. She realized her own inability to cope with the situation, and realized too that if she insisted on accompanying him, she would merely handicap him and interfere with his plans.

"You'll be careful, won't you?"

He smiled fleetingly.

"Sure," he answered. He hitched up his belt and shifted his holster again so that the jutting butt of his Colt was directly below his right hand. "Look, Beth. Mebbe you'd better stay in town t'night, huh? I don't like th' idea o' you ridin' out in th' darkness all by y'self, not th' way things are happenin' now. You close up shop at sundown, same's we allus do, get y'self somethin' to eat, an' then hustle up t' my room at th' Standard an' stay there. If I know you're awright, that'll be one thing less f'r me t' worry about."

"Then you don't expect to be back tonight, do you?"

He looked at her for a moment, then shook his head.

"No," he said.

Her eyes probed his face.

"You think there'll be more raids?"

"Yep," he replied. "But they won't be just ord'nary raids, Beth. They're all part uva scheme Quarles's cooked up. This hull thing's got a fine touch to it, somethin' ord'nary rustlers don't go in for. That's why I figger it's all part uv somethin' bigger'n just cattle rustlin' an' raids. But, at th' rate things are happenin', I figger everything'll come out in th' open soon enough, an' then we'll all know what's b'hind these goin's on. Look: Fox's, Hockett's and one more place are all pretty much grouped t'gether, ain't they? Who owns th' third one?"

"Larry Parker."

"Uh-huh. Couldn't seem t' r'member that name f'r th' life o' me."

"Is that where you'll be tonight—at Parker's?"

"That's one o' th' places I'll be at. I aim t' cover as much ground as I can. Wa—al, reckon I'd better get goin'. Can't do anything hangin' aroun' here, y'know. You watch out f'r y'self, y'hear?"

He turned and strode to the door, opened it, looked back at her over his shoulder, then closed the door behind him.

It was one of the longest nights Beth Richards had ever known. Actually it was hardly more than four hours since she had gone into Canavan's room, but it seemed like years to her. Now it was eleven o'clock, and after an evening of alternating between the edge of the bed and the chair near the window, she trudged wearily to the door and tried the lock for the seventh time. Satisfied that the bolt was drawn as far as it would go, she turned out the light and groped her way to the window. She pushed the curtain aside, drew the chair closer and seated herself. Resting her arms on the window sill, she looked down into the street below. It was a dark night and she felt uneasy. Then, too, there was no activity in the street, no lights anywhere save at the corner, in the "K. C." She could hear loud voices and even louder laughter, and occasionally she could hear someone playing the piano. Somehow the noise from the "K. C." attracted her and she moved her chair so that she could see the yellow-lighted doorway.

Canavan came into her thoughts. She could see him now and she seemed to be following him with her eyes. He was so tall and broad-shouldered and he walked with the easy gait of a trained athlete. He seemed to come closer to her for a moment and she fancied she could see his eyes; they were light and gay and they crinkled when he laughed. Then he was suddenly grim-faced and tight-lipped and his eyes were steely and cold.

She wondered about him, wondered where he had come from, what his life had been like up to his arrival in Logan, wondered what his family was like. Her thoughts went back over the years. She was a little girl again, and there was a little boy, a redheaded boy named Johnny Andrews, who lived near by. She could picture him so clearly: he had a mop of unruly red hair, a cowlick, a face full of freckles, a little upturned nose that seemed to wrinkle when he grinned. Johnny Andrews had never liked her. He'd played with her on occasion, when his mother had brought him over, leading him by the hand, but as soon as his mother turned away, Johnny would scamper off as fast as his sturdy young legs would carry him. Out of curiosity, Beth recalled, she had followed him one day. He swung wide of his house, reached the rear of the Andrews barn, then hustled inside. Beth had followed at his heels; she found a ladder in a far corner of the barn, made her way up its rungs to the hayloft and, worming her way forward on her hands and knees, she found Johnny playing at his favorite game. He'd made a wooden box covered with canvas serve as a prairie schooner; atop a tall heap of hay he lay sprawled out on his stomach, rifle in hand, guarding the covered wagon from afar. From time to time he would stiffen and grunt a single word—"Injun." Then the rifle would snap upward to his shoulder. "Bing!" he would say with satisfaction. "Gotcha!" Then he would lower his rifle and relax.

Beth recalled that she'd come away from the Andrews barn saddened and disappointed. To think that anyone, even a freckle-faced boy, would prefer to fight an "Injun" war rather than play real games—well, she didn't really know what to make of it. Then her thoughts shifted again. Johnny Andrews was a young man. He came around the barn just as Beth appeared carrying a cake her mother had baked for Mrs. Andrews. Somehow she could never recall just what had happened. Johnny cornered her and, though she protested, even seeking to use the cake as a barrier between them, he kissed her. He avoided her after that until it reached the point where she sought him out. There was a blank space in her memory then; that was probably when Johnny left home. But he returned a year later and tragedy followed.

He was a skillful horseman and he made riding appear easy, even when he was breaking a wild horse. She was perched on the top rail of the Andrews corral one morning when Johnny tramped in and locked the gate behind him. In a far corner of the corral a lone, evil-eyed horse waited. The horse stood still while Johnny swung his saddle over the animal's back. Johnny had barely slid into the saddle when the horse bolted and in a snorting rage plunged headlong into the side of the corral. Beth screamed in terror and other punchers appeared on the run. They lifted the broken body of Johnny Andrews and carried him into the house. Beth ran beside him, holding his hand. She recalled that he'd opened his eyes, looked up at her and smiled; he was silent and motionless the next minute. In the morning Johnny Andrews was dead.

Now she was again watching a little redheaded boy with an upturned nose set in a freckled face. Strangely enough, it wasn't Johnny Andrews's face at all; it was John Canavan's! The face and the body below it grew larger and Canavan appeared again, a man, striding out of nowhere, tall and erect and easy-gaited. She wondered whether there was a little girl somewhere—of course she'd be full-grown now—who'd wanted him to play with her as she had wanted Johnny Andrews; she wondered, too, whether Canavan had once turned to the little girl and said scornfully, as Johnny Andrews had said: "Girls? Heck, I just don't like 'em that's all."

Beth smiled gently with the deep understanding that comes with maturity. She sighed. She was terribly tired now and her eyes were heavy. Her head came down a bit, nodding, drooping. An unfamiliar face came into her thoughts, crowding everything else out of focus; it was a pretty face. Beth was certain she had never seen the girl before. Beth eyed her with increasing resentment. The girl's lips moved and Beth, straining to the extreme, barely managed to hear what she was saying.

"Johnny," the voice murmured. "Johnny Canavan! I'm waiting for you, Johnny. Please come back to me, Johnny."

Instantly the vision vanished, but its appearance had left

Beth troubled. She had accepted Canavan's services without thought or question; somehow, too, she hadn't given a thought to the possibility that somewhere in that vast beyond that was his earlier life a girl might be waiting for him to return. Now she was disturbed over it. Her face clouded. Her eyes closed and her head sank into her pillowing arms. Presently she sighed again, then she seemed to settle a bit, and she was asleep.

There was a sudden deafening crash of thunder and Beth stirred. Just as suddenly, she jerked and her head came up. For a moment she was rigid with bewilderment and fright. Finally she moved and looked quickly in the direction of the "K. C.," but there was no light visible in the café. She got to her feet, leaned out over the window sill and looked down the street. She heard a man's voice cry out, and her heart pounded up into her throat. There was a sharp clatter of horses' hoofs, and as she watched with fear-widened eyes, six horsemen came racing up the street. They thundered past the Standard at a whirlwind gallop, swept past the darkened "K. C.," dashed out of town and disappeared in the night.

She turned and plunged toward the door, fumbled with the lock, finally managed to pull the bolt free, flung open the door and burst out of the room. She fled along the narrow hallway and raced down the flight of stairs. Fortunately the front door was unlocked and she opened it with a single twist of her wrist and stepped into the street. She dashed out toward the middle of the street, avoiding the shadow-draped structures as if she feared that unseen hands might reach out and seize her. She saw the indistinguishable figure of a man appear out of a doorway, and almost instantly she recognized him.

"Mr. Comerford!" she panted.

He gave her a brief glance over his shoulder, then went on and darted into the bank. Beth quickened her pace; she came running up presently and stopped in the open doorway. Comerford had just finished lighting a lamp. He held it in his hand and its yellow light formed an arc over the floor, on which were strewn papers and limp canvas bags with their tying strings trailing behind them. Beth's eyes ranged past Comerford. She screamed, and Comerford's eyes followed her pointing finger. In a corner behind an overturned desk lay the huddled figure of a man. Beth knew at once that it was Colonel Wynn.

Canavan's horse whinnied softly and stopped. The redheaded youth eased himself in the saddle and looked up. In the dim light of dawn, everything about him seemed stark cold—even the sprawled-out body of a man on the ground some twenty feet ahead of him. Canavan swung himself out of the saddle and stamped his legs. The long hours in the saddle had stiffened him. He shifted his holster, went swiftly forward and, bending over the man, turned him over on his back. A single glance told him that the man was dead; there were two bullet holes, already black-rimmed, in his shirt front, and a third one just below his throat. Canavan climbed to his feet.

His horse whinnied again and Canavan looked up. There was a grass-muffled hoofbeat, and a riderless horse trotted up, slowed to a walk and went directly to the motionless body on the ground. Canavan patted the horse's neck; the animal nudged the dead man with his nose and whinnied softly when there was no response.

"Tough luck, ol' feller," Canavan said to the horse. "Now, if you'll kinda lend a hand, mebbe we c'n get 'im home f'r you."

Canavan bent down again, lifted the man, swung him upward over his shoulder, then with an effort managed to get him into the saddle. Fortunately the man's lariat still hung on the saddle horn. Holding the man steady with one hand, Canavan lashed him to the saddle. At a signal from him, Canavan's horse trotted up. The tall youth mounted and caught up the other horse's bridle. Presently they rode slowly away toward Parker's place. It was lighter now and the veil that had stood between dawn and day was whisked away. The awakening sun appeared on the horizon and there was a general stirring on the earth. A light breeze rustled the grass and brush, and a bird, flashing across the sky, wheeled and swooped down for a look at the limp, bound figure on the trailing horse, circled, then wheeled again and sped away southward.

6. Angels with Clipped Wings ★

IT WAS about nine in the morning when Canavan rode into town. There were a few men idling in front of the "K. C.," and they looked up when they heard the clatter of hoofbeats, eyed him, turned slowly and watched him silently as he jogged past. He rode down the street, pulled up presently in front of the office, dismounted stiffly, tied up his horse at the rail, hitched up his pants and sauntered up to the door, opened it and halted in the doorway. Beth was there, seated behind the battered desk, but she was not alone. There were half a dozen men in the office, too, and Canavan's questioning eyes ranged over them. They in turn looked at him—Ed Hockett and Will Davis, who were leaning against one wall; Matt Fox, bristly and angry-faced, who had taken possession of the only other chair besides Beth's and who sat astride it with the same grimness with which he doubtless straddled his horse; the Gillens and a man whose face seemed only vaguely familiar, who stood with their backs to the opposite wall. Beth, Canavan noted, was unusually quiet and kept her eyes averted.

"H'm," he said lightly, forgetting for the moment that he was too tired to be particularly sociable. "Looks like a meeting. This somethin' private, or c'n anybody get in on it?"

"We've been holding things up for you," Beth answered without looking up. He had already sensed that something was amiss; now he was certain of it. Mechanically he squared his shoulders. Fox, he assumed with good reason, would be the one he would have to take on.

"That's right, Canavan," Hockett said. "Come in an' close that door b'hind you like a good feller."

"Sure," Canavan replied.

He stepped inside, pulled the door toward him and sidestepped it as it swung in its arc. It swept past him and he caught it in time to prevent it from slamming, closed it quietly, then sauntered forward and halted in front of the desk. His big hands dangled for a moment; then he hooked his thumbs in his belt and waited patiently for whatever was to come. When Hockett coughed lightly and cleared his throat, Canavan turned toward him.

"Canavan," the big rancher began.

"Yeah?"

Hockett seemed a bit uncomfortable with Canavan's steady eyes on him and he coughed again behind a big hand. Fox twisted around in his chair and looked up at Hockett and scowled.

"Come on," he said impatiently. "Come on an' let's get this business over with."

"Canavan," Hockett began again, "we're here b'cause we've d'cided that somethin's gotta be done."

"Awright," Canavan said in reply. "So far, y'know it's been just Beth an' me against Quarles an' his outfit. Now if you fellers are ready t' step in b'side us, mebbe we c'n really get somewheres."

Fox grunted loudly; actually it was intended as a voicing of his scorn. Hockett turned his head slightly and looked down at him, then looked up at Canavan again.

"These here raids that Quarles's been pullin' off on us," he went on, "wa—al, we've stood just about as much o' th'm as we c'n. Then, havin' th' bank robbed last night was th' pay-off. It was about eleven o'clock, wasn't it, Beth?"

"It was probably nearer eleven-thirty," Beth answered.

Fox jerked his head up.

"What in blazes does it matter what time it was?" he demanded. "Th' point is th' bank was robbed an' we lost money."

Hockett frowned and drew a deep breath.

"Th' way we got it fr'm Beth, Canavan," he continued, "it seems like you've been th' hull works 'round here. If that's th' case, then we want you t' know what we're figgerin' on doin'."

"Awright, Ed," Fox said again, "you've given 'im th' salve. Now come t' th' point an' tell 'im what's what."

"Mebbe you think you c'n tell 'im better'n I c'n," Hockett said with annoyance in his voice.

"You're damned tootin' I c'n," Fox said quickly. "An' I'm gonna." He got to his feet and slung the chair away. It collided with the wall and he glared at it for a moment. "Look, Canavan, we've had seven raids pulled off on us. Five o' our men've been shot an' four o' th' five are dead. Then we lost fourteen hundred head o' cattle. To top it all off, th' bank was robbed last night."

"Them figures o' yourn were yesterday's," Canavan said quietly.

"Huh? What d'you mean?"

"Parker got it last night, so that makes th' count eight raids."

"Oh, yeah?"

"One o' his men was killed," Canavan continued, "an' th' raiders run off more'n two hundred o' his best steers."

"So that's why he didn't show up here t'day," Fox said, shaking his head. He raised his eyes again to meet Canavan's. "These men know me better'n you do, an' they c'n tell you that I ain't th' kind that gives up anything without fightin' f'r it first. But th' way I see this thing, we ain't got a chance. We've gotta sit in on a game an' take th' cards that are bein' dealt us fr'm a stacked deck, an' we can't do a damned thing about it."

"What d'you s'ggest?"

"Wal—al, we've either gotta take what Quarles's dishin' out t' us an' go broke or—"

"Or what?"

"Or pull in our horns," Fox concluded.

"What's that s'pposed t' mean?"

"Matt means that th' longer we go on opposin' Quarles," Hockett explained, "th' worse off we're gonna be. He thinks Beth oughta quit bein' sheriff an' that we oughta fade outa th' picture an' let Quarles put in 'is own sheriff. Mebbe then he'll kinda lay off us."

"I see," said Canavan. " 'Course it ain't f'r me t' tell you fellers what t' do. It's your money, your men an' your cattle that you're losin', so that gives you th' right t' do whatever you want. But don't you see that by givin' up now you're playin' right into Quarles's hands?"

Fox snorted angrily.

"What I want t' do makes good sense t' me," he said curtly, even defiantly. "If we quit standin' up t' Quarles, we got a damned good chance o' hangin' on to what we got left, an' with that we c'n build up again."

Canavan shrugged his shoulders.

"Suit y'self, mister. Like I said b'fore, I'm on'y an outsider lookin' in. But what makes you fellers think Quarles's gonna call off his dogs an' let you live in peace? How d'you know he ain't gonna go right on an' even take your ranches away fr'm you?"

"That's r'diculous!" Hockett said loudly. "What'n blazes would he want with 'em?"

"Same thing he wants with your cattle!" Canavan retorted. "Right fr'm th' beginnin' it was plain's day that it was gonna be either him or you fellers who won out. Now he's found out that you fellers can't take it an' that you won't even fight back, so he's ridin' high. He's gonna bust every last one o' you an', take my word f'r it, soon's you b'gin t' knuckle down t' him, he'll ride over you like you were dirt. Beth—"

She raised her head and answered him with her eyes.

"Beth," he said again, "looks t' me like th' on'y thing f'r you t' do is quit, an' I think you oughta do it right here an' now. 'Stead o' gettin' backin' fr'm th' ones who made you sheriff, you're gettin' th' cold shoulder. An' now that I'm on th' subject, mebbe a little plain speakin' would be in order."

Hockett coughed again lightly and Canavan whirled.

"Hockett," he demanded, "who cooked up th' idea o' makin' Beth sheriff?"

The burly rancher colored.

"Oh, I dunno. I s'ppose you might say we all kinda had a hand in it," he answered lamely.

"I don't b'lieve that," Canavan said coldly. "It sounds like you or mebbe Fox got th' bright idea an' got th' others t' agree to it. But that ain't important right now. What is important is that now I c'n understan' what was b'hind th' hull thing. None o' you had th' guts t' take th' job o' sheriff after seein' what happened t' John Richards, so you cooked up th' scheme that mebbe you could shove Beth down Quarles's throat an' that bein' she was a woman, he'd b'have 'imself an' leave 'er alone. Yeah, that was it, awright. An' I think it was th' lousiest trick ever pulled off on anyone, 'specially a woman. An' you fellers were s'pposed t' be John Richards's friends. If there's any way o' him gettin' wind o' th' deal handed 'is daughter by 'is friends, then I'll bet he's burnin' up down b'low."

"Mister," Fox said heavily, "I don't like you. F'r that matter, I didn't like you th' first time I saw you. Now I know I'll never like you. My advice t' you is—"

"Who'n hell is askin' you f'r advice?" Canavan demanded fiercely. "You ain't even got th' guts t' fight f'r what's yourn, an' you're gonna give me advice? Why, you yeller-bellied ol' coot—"

There was a roar from Fox. He backed away a bit, jerked his right arm backward and sought to draw his gun. Big Ed Hockett, wheeling with surprising swiftness for one of his bulk, crashed against him, pinned him to the wall and gripped his gun wrist in one huge hand.

"Leggo, Ed!" Fox yelled, struggling to break Hockett's hold on him. "Leggo, y'hear? Gimme just one chance an' I'll blast that skunk apart!"

Canavan had not moved.

"You'd better take Grandpa's gun away fr'm 'im, Hockett," he said coldly. "That's th' second time he's gone f'r it against me an' I'm gettin' tired uv it. Next time he tries it, I won't be r'sponsible f'r what happens to 'im. I'm li'ble t' f'rget he's so old an' take it away fr'm 'im m'self an' beat 'is brains out with it."

"Yeah?" Fox sputtered, still struggling. "Lemme tell you somethin', mister. I'm givin' you fair warnin' that next time I run into you, I'm gonna go f'r my gun an' I'm gonna start shootin'!"

Canavan laughed scornfully.

"On'y thing you c'n shoot off is that big mouth o' yourn," he said. He turned to Beth. "Come on. Speak your piece an' let's get outa here. S'me fresh air'll do us both good."

Beth hesitated for a moment. He shrugged his shoulders, turned on his heel, strode to the door and threw it open. Then he looked back over his shoulder.

"Beth," he called, "I'll be over at that Comerford feller's place. You c'n find me there."

The door slammed behind him. It opened again in another moment and he poked his head inside.

"Here," he said coldly. "Here's my badge. Pin it on th' seat o' that ol' buzzard's pants. That's where it b'longs now!"

A silver star came flashing through space. It struck the floor, skidded over it and came to an abrupt stop when it collided with Fox's boot. They heard the door slam again.

Henry Comerford was idling in the open doorway of the *Bugle* office when Canavan came striding up to him. The pudgy man with the twinkling eyes looked up at him and grinned.

"H'm," he said. "You look mad enough t' eat nails. Who's been doin' nasty things to Mrs. Canavan's favorite son?"

"Never mind that f'r now. I understan' th' bank was robbed last night. That right?"

Comerford nodded.

"They get away with much?"

"Practically everything."

"How 'bout th' old feller—that Colonel Wynn?"

"Oh, he's all right now," Comerford answered. "He got a nasty wallop over the head, but he'll be as good as new in another day or two."

"Look," Canavan said, "I got somethin' I'd like t' talk t' you about—private, y'know."

Comerford looked up at him again and nodded. Then he turned and led the way to the rear of the newspaper office. He swung a chair around and Canavan took it and stood it against a wall. When Comerford brought another chair forward and sat down on it, Canavan seated himself too.

"Where's your badge?" the newspaper publisher asked.

Canavan scowled darkly.

"Gave it back," he replied. "Tol' Hockett t' pin it on th' seat o' Matt Fox's pants."

"Oh, so that's what's eating you! What happened?"

"Nuthin' much 'cept that th' ranchers are quittin' th' fight against Quarles."

"No!"

Canavan nodded grimly.

"They're quittin' in th' hopes that mebbe Quarles'll lay offa th'm an' let th'm alone."

"But what about Beth—and you?"

"Beth an' me are outa jobs. They're leavin' th' job o' sheriff open as a peace offerin' t' Quarles. They got 'n idea that if they quit opposin' 'im an' if they let 'im name 'is own sheriff, everything'll be peaceful again."

"But how do they know that Quarles will be satisfied with that balm?"

"That's th' same question I asked, an' that's what started th' rumpus."

Comerford arose, turned and paced the floor.

"It's sheer madness," he said over his shoulder. "You can't compromise with evil and live with it on equal terms."

"That's th' way I feel about it," Canavan said. "I know Quarles's kind. They're ornery an' greedy, an' th' worst thing anyone c'n do is t' try t' make terms with 'em. Mister, 'less I miss my guess—an' I'm willin' t' bet that I won't—there's gonna be hell on earth in Logan with Quarles in c'mmand o' things."

"You have a plan?" Comerford asked.

"Yep."

"What is it?"

"In case you hafta move them presses o' yourn in a hurry, c'n you do it?"

"I've done it before," Comerford answered grimly. "In the middle of the night, too."

"Awright then. You an' me are gonna take up th' fight against Quarles. You're gonna do your share o' th' fightin' with words printed on paper. I'm gonna do th' real kind o' fightin'. T'gether we c'n put a crimp in Mister Quarles's plans."

There was a new gleam in Comerford's eyes.

"Go on," he said.

"First off," Canavan began, "I'm leavin' Logan f'r a couple o' days. In the meantime you go t' work cookin' up s'me editorials that'll burn th' ears offa Quarles. I oughta be back, say in three days. Th' minute I'm back, we're goin' t' work on Quarles. But you're gonna hafta be ready t' move th' minute I give you th' word."

"I understand fully. I'll have the editorials ready."

Canavan got to his feet.

"But aren't you going to tell me any more of your plan?" Comerford asked.

"Haven't got it all worked out yet. I know what we're gonna do. Now all I've gotta do is figger out how we c'n do it."

Comerford got to his feet.

"But you'll be back, won't you?"

"I will 'less I'm dead."

They shook hands gravely, then went to the door.

"Oh, yeah," Canavan said. "Somethin' I nearly f'rgot. Keep 'n eye on Beth f'r me, will you?"

"I'll be glad to. Incidentally, does she know anything of this plan of yours?"

"Nope. She doesn't know anything about it at all."

"Suppose she asks questions?"

Canavan grinned down at him.

"You know all the words an' how t' use 'em. You oughta be able t' think up 'n answer f'r any question she c'n ask."

He nodded and went out. Comerford, following him with his eyes, saw him go directly to his horse in front of Beth's office, mount, wheel and come loping down the street. When Canavan came abreast of the *Bugle* office, he did not turn his head. He settled himself in the saddle, spurred his horse and sent him bounding away. Beth came out of her office and caught a glimpse of Canavan as he dashed past the "K. C." As she watched, he swerved and raced out of town. Beth was motionless for a moment; then she turned slowly and trudged down the alley that led to the lean-to behind the office. She reappeared a few minutes later astride her horse and rode down the street. As she neared the "K. C.," Quarles appeared in the doorway. He smiled and touched the brim of his hat, but there was no acknowledgment from Beth. She rode slowly out of town, a slender figure of a lonely girl with a bowed head.

7. Quarles's Law ★

HENRY COMERFORD pulled back the bolt on his front door, yawned, stretched himself, scratched the top of his head, hitched up his suspenders and finally opened the door. He looked up with surprise when he found himself facing a man armed with a rifle who was leaning against the doorjamb.

"Oh!" Comerford said. He rubbed his nose with the back of his hand. "Didn't expect to find anyone waiting on my doorstep this early in the morning. What c'n I do f'r you, partner?"

The man, a tall, lean fellow with a wide mouth, large ears and huge, bony hands, pointed to a silver star that was pinned to his shirt front.

"Y'see that?" he asked.

"Huh? Oh, yeah! Deputy sheriff, eh?"

"That's right. Now look, mister. Accordin' t' th' law, nob'dy c'n do business in Logan 'less he's got one o' them there permits. Get th' idea?"

"Vaguely. Just when was that law passed?"

"Last night."

"You don't say! And who passed it, might I ask?"

"Oh, you c'n ask awright. That ain't against th' law; leastways it ain't been up t' now."

"Then I suppose I'd better take advantage of the situation while I've still got the opportunity. Who passed that rather curious law, my friend?"

The man grinned and shifted his weight from one leg to the other.

"Quarles," he answered. "He's runnin' Logan now, y'know."

"So I gathered," Comerford commented dryly. "So he's the financial genius who cooked up this new wrinkle in the fine art of corralling loose dollars, eh? An' what does a permit cost?"

"Twenty bucks."

"Twenty, eh?" Comerford repeated. "Cheaper to stay closed."

The man grinned again; his teeth were large and yellowish.

"No deal, partner," he said. "Either you get y'self a permit like th' law says or out you go an' someb'dy else with a permit comes in an' takes over."

"That's very interesting. Evidently your Mister Quarles hasn't overlooked any angles, has he?"

"Nope. What'll it be, mister?"

"Must I give you an answer immediately, or may I take a little time for deliberation?"

"Oh, reckon I c'n wait till th' same time t'morrow mornin'."

"Thank you."

"That's awright. Just lock up again like a good feller an' I'll come by again t'morrow."

"But—"

"No business till you get y'self that permit. That's what th' law says."

Comerford frowned, stepped back inside, slammed the door shut and drove the bolt home. The man grinned, turned away, looked back over his shoulder, then went on down the street. When he came to the next store, he stopped, peered inside, hitched up his belt and went in. A farm wagon rolled into town, braked and creaked to a stop in front of the Standard Hotel. Two men climbed down and marched into the hotel. When they came out some ten or fifteen minutes later, there was no sign of the wagon. The older of the two men, a middle-aged man with a windburned face and a drooping mustache, looked up and down the street; his companion, a husky and considerably younger man, seemed too surprised or puzzled to do anything helpful. He scratched his head, then his nose.

"I'll be doggoned!" he muttered half aloud. "I'll be doggoned!"

Mother Jones was standing in the doorway of her place. She watched them a minute longer.

"Mister Carroll!" she called shortly.

The mustached man turned around.

"Huh? Oh, h'llo, Missus Jones," he answered.

"You looking for something?"

"Yeah, sure," Carroll said quickly. "You see anything uv a wagon out here?"

"Oh, was that your wagon?"

"It was," Carroll said, "an' so were th' two horses hitched to it."

"A couple of men drove it away."

The rancher's eyes widened.

"Huh? What d'you mean, they drove it away?" he demanded.

"Maybe you oughta go see that new sheriff o' ours," Mother Jones replied. "He oughta be able t' tell you what happened to your wagon."

"New sheriff?" Carroll repeated. He looked at his companion; the latter arched his eyebrows. "Y'mean Beth Richards ain't got th' job any more?"

"She quit yest'day," Mother Jones said. "Understand Quarles took it over an' put that man o' his, Murray, in her place."

"Wa—al, what d'you know! Come on, Ted. Let's go see that feller Murray an' hear what he's gotta say 'bout this business. An' he better have plenty t' say, too. Nob'dy's gonna run off with my wagon an' get away with it! Come on!"

The two men, turning away as one, strode briskly down the street and went into the sheriff's office. Quarles and Murray were sitting at the desk. There were three other men standing near the door. Carroll, glancing at them, noted that all three were wearing silver stars. Murray looked up. He nudged Quarles, and the latter raised his head.

"Howdy," Murray said. "Oh, you're Carroll o' th' Box-C—right?"

"That's right," Carroll said gruffly, making no attempt to veil his annoyance. "Left m' wagon standin' outside o' th' Standard Hotel, an' when I come out again, mebbe fifteen minutes after, th' wagon was gone. Know anything about it?"

There was no immediate answer. Murray started to speak, when Quarles, moving in his chair, kicked him under the desk. The newly appointed lawman frowned and snapped his jaws shut. Carroll evidently failed to notice it, for he leaned over the desk and went on with his story.

"Understan' fr'm Mother Jones," he continued, "that a couple o' fellers wearin' badges come along an' drove it away. What'n thunder d'you make o' that?"

"Keep your shirt on, Carroll," Quarles said. "If you'da been here last night, you'da knowed there was a new law passed."

"What kind o' law?"

"Oh, just a gen'ral nuisance law."

"A what kind o' law?"

"A nuisance law," Quarles repeated. "F'r instance, we wanna keep Logan's streets fr'm gettin' cluttered up with wagons an' such, so we passed a law 'gainst it. Now, accordin' t' th' law, all wagons are s'pposed t' be left a mile outside o' town or in th' space we've set aside f'r 'em b'hind Bailey's stables. 'Course there's a small charge f'r leavin' 'em there, at Bailey's, y'understand. Two bucks f'r each horse an' one buck apiece f'r waterin' 'em."

"Wa—al, I'll be damned!"

"Accordin' t' th' law," Quarles went on calmly, "you're fined ten bucks f'r breakin' it."

Carroll's head jerked up. His mustache stiffened.

"Oh, yeah?"

"Yeah," Quarles went on. "An' five dollars extra f'r every hour after th' first hour."

Carroll blinked and swallowed hard.

"An' if your outfit ain't r'deemed b'fore sundown," Quarles said unhurriedly, "th' law takes it over an' sells it at public auction th' next mornin'. You ain't allowed t' bid f'r it. That's t' keep things on th' up-an'-up, y'understand. So what'll it be, Carroll? Gonna pay up an' r'member t' obey th' law th' next time, or do we sell your outfit and take th' fine an' th' extras outa what we sell it f'r?"

"How much now?" Carroll demanded through gritted teeth.

"Wa—al, let's see now. Ten bucks f'r th' fine, five bucks f'r every hour or part uv 'n hour, an' one buck apiece f'r waterin' your two horses. Seventeen bucks in all."

"Awright, I'm payin' it," Carroll said. "But I'm addin' this t' this hold-up, mister. One o' these days I'm gonna cut seventeen bucks' worth o' hide offa you. That's a promise."

"Sure," Quarles said. "Where's th' dough?"

The cattleman dug into his pocket, pulled out a canvas bag, untied it, counted out seventeen silver dollars and tossed them on the desk.

"There y'are," he said gruffly.

Quarles laughed softly.

"Awright, boys," he called. "You fellers take Mister Carroll an' his hired hand over t' Bailey's an' see to it that they get their outfit. So long, Carroll."

"So long, hell!" Carroll flung over his shoulder as he stormed out. "I'll be back t' see you, mister, an' it won't be a social call that I'll be makin'!"

Quarles's laugh followed him out to the street.

It was evening, about eight-thirty, when three horsemen loped into town. They rode past the "K. C.," returning the hostile stares of a group of Quarles's men who were idling in front of the café. They clattered down the street, pulled up in front of a small, dimly lighted saloon, dismounted and tied up their horses at the rail, and sauntered inside. It was nearly nine o'clock when they emerged, jerked to an abrupt stop and looked at one another.

"Hey!" one man said quickly. "Where'n hell are our horses, huh?"

"That's just what I was gonna ask," another man said. "I'm doggoned sure we left 'em out here an' that we tied 'em up."

" 'Course!" the first man said.

"Wa—al," the third man said, "they ain't here now. They've just done an' gone."

"Oh, yeah?" the first man said. "Horses don't just up an' go off. Not when they're tied up. You fellers go up the street an' have a look aroun'. I'll go th' other way. If you see anything, holler, an' I'll come a-runnin'."

There were half a dozen men lounging in a darkened doorway across the street. They watched the punchers for a minute and waited until the cowmen parted. Then four of the men hitched up their belts, cut across the street diagonally and fell in behind the two punchers. Two men followed the first puncher. He turned around quickly when he heard footsteps behind him.

"S'matter, partner?" one man asked casually. "Lose somethin'?"

"Yeah," the puncher replied. "Three horses wearin' th' Box-O brand."

"Oh, were they yourn?"

"Damned right they were, an' if I run into th' skunk that run 'em off, I'll give 'im a dose o' lead poisonin' he ain't never gonna get over. You fellers see anything o' th'm or see anybody ridin' off with th'm?"

"Yeah, come t' think uv it, I kinda r'member seein' some feller ridin' away with three horses roped t'gether."

"Yuh did?" the puncher said quickly. "When was it, an' which way'd they go?"

"Oh, it wasn't more'n fifteen minutes ago."

"An'—?"

"Seems t' me he went off that way," the man continued, nodding toward the corner. "Come on, we'll go 'long with you an' help you get 'em back."

The three men, with the puncher in the middle, started away briskly. Suddenly the puncher stopped.

"Wait a minute," he said. "You fellers new 'round here? I don't r'member ever seein' you in Logan b'fore. What's your outfit?"

"Look, partner, you want them horses o' yourn?"

"Yeah, sure."

"Then s'ppose we cut out th' gab an' just keep goin' like we was."

They went on again, though the puncher appeared more than just a bit uneasy about the situation. He stole glances at his companions but they pretended not to notice. When they came abreast of the sheriff's office, they stopped. The puncher looked at them quickly, questioningly; he raised his eyes to the sign that hung over the doorway.

"This is th' place," one man said.

The puncher started to back away. He collided with the muzzle of a gun and stopped in his tracks.

"Open th' door, Gibby," the man behind the gun said briefly.

The office door was flung open. The puncher caught a fleeting glimpse of half a dozen men inside the place; then he was shoved in. The gun dug deeper into his back and he moved ahead faster, halting a second time in front of the desk that stood in the middle of the office. There were two men behind it and he recognized them at once. His eyes shifted momentarily, ranging over the other men in the room. Their faces were vaguely familiar and he noted in that moment that each man wore a silver star on his shirt front. Quarles sat back in his chair.

"What's th' matter with this feller, Del?" he asked presently. "What's he done?"

Just then more men crowded into the office. The puncher stole a quick look at them over his shoulder. They were his companions, and behind them were four men he had never seen before.

"Wa—al, looks like this is our night f'r gettin' comp'ny," Quarles said. "What's th' charge 'gainst these fellers?"

"Found th'm roamin' lookin' f'r some horses," a man said from the doorway.

"I see," Quarles said. "Where you fellers from?"

"Th' Box-O," the first puncher answered stiffly.

"Uh-huh. An' what's your name?"

"Swain. Them two are Hilly an' O'Brien. Now s'ppose you tell us what'n hell's goin' on 'round here. You got our horses?"

"Sure we got 'em," Quarles said calmly.

"Awright then. Trot 'em out, will yuh? We got places t' go."

"They ain't yourn any more."

"They ain't, eh? Mebbe you'd like t' tell me whose they are then."

"They b'long t' th' town o' Logan," Quarles went on evenly. "Accordin' t' th' law, horses left unattended in th' streets o' th' town are subject t' confiscation."

"Come again?" Swain said.

Quarles laughed softly.

"Sure," he said. "In plainer English it means that if you leave a horse or wagon or anything else in th' street, you're plumb outa luck. Th' town takes it over."

"What are you tryin' t' give me, huh?"

"I'm on'y tellin' you what th' law says," Quarles replied.

Swain scowled darkly. His eyes shifted away from Quarles; then they returned.

"But bein' that this is your first offense," Quarles went on, "mebbe we oughta go easy on you."

"Sure," Murray said. "We don't wanna rub it in."

Quarles looked at him and laughed again.

"Awright, Tex," he said. "We'll let 'em off with a fine. But next time it'll be diff'rent."

"You're damned right it will!" Swain replied, gritting his teeth. "Next time we find our horses gone, we'll go lookin' f'r 'em with our guns in our hands. Now trot 'em out!"

"They'll cost you ten bucks apiece."

"Ten bucks, hell!"

"Awright," Quarles said calmly, "if that's th' way you feel about it, reckon it's awright with us. Take th'm away, boys. Mebbe Mister Swain'll feel diff'rent 'bout things in th' mornin'."

Rough hands seized the punchers and dragged them out of the office.

"Now, then," Quarles said, "Bennett, you get your boys t'gether an' get goin'. Where's Kull?"

"Saw him over at th' 'K. C.' earlier in th' evenin'," a man answered.

"His bunch don't head out till midnight," Murray said.

"That's right," Quarles said. "Danko, you all set?"

"Sure, Boss," a tall, dark man replied. "We pull outa Logan 'bout 'leven-thirty. Leastways, that's th' way you figgered it this mornin'."

"'Leven-thirty is right," Murray said. "'Less you wanna change it, Dan."

"Nope," Quarles said, "we'll stick t' th' schedule. But don't any o' you fellers in charge f'rget t' send me word how things go. Awright, Bennett. Beat it."

8. Shadows on Horseback ★

It was midnight. A cool, breathless, murmuring breeze that carried the indistinguishable hum of voices in its folds swept over the moonlit range. Shadowy horsemen, probably a dozen of them, rode swiftly over the range and swerved southward for a mile or two. Then, when darkened buildings suddenly loomed up ahead of them, they separated and swung away. Most of the band raced toward the low, squat, ungainly bunkhouse. The others pulled up in front of the ranch house, dismounted, dashed up the porch steps and burst inside.

Will Davis rolled over on his back, grunted and opened his eyes reluctantly when yellow lamplight flamed and flooded his bedroom. He blinked, made a wry face and threw up his right arm to shade his heavy-lidded eyes.

"Hey!" he sputtered. "What'n blazes is th' idea, huh?"

There were three men standing around his bed. He knew, in that one fleeting look, that he had never seen any of them before. There were leveled guns in their hands, too, and when he glanced at the rifle he had laid against the bedstead, their eyes followed his. One of the men stepped forward quickly, caught up the rifle and turned away with it. Another man moved closer to Davis. The rancher sat up.

"Reckon you're Davis," the man said. "That right?"

Will nodded.

"Yeah, but—"

The man's Colt snapped upward and Davis's jaws clamped shut.

"We'll do th' talkin'," the man said dryly. "You do th' listenin' an' you'll live longer. Davis, accordin' t' th' records, you owe Logan nine hundred bucks f'r taxes—last year's an' this. We've come f'r th' dough."

"This is one helluva time t'—" Will sputtered. He frowned and closed his mouth again when the muzzle of the Colt seemed to yawn at him. Presently his head jerked upward defiantly. "Nine hundred bucks, did you say? Mister, you're plumb locoed. It was two hundred f'r last year an' two hundred f'r this year. That makes four hundred th' way I figger it."

The man grinned down at him.

"There's a little matter uv a fine you're overlookin'," he said coolly.

"Huh?"

"You've been fined five hundred bucks f'r not payin' up last year's taxes."

"Fine?" Davis echoed. "What d'you mean there's a fine? When did that all come about? An' who's doin' th' finin'?"

The man grinned again.

"Quarles," he answered simply. "What'll it be, mister? You payin' up or ain't you?"

Davis frowned deeply.

"I can't pay any part uv it," he replied. "All th' cash I had was in th' bank. It's gone, same's everybody else's."

The man shrugged his shoulders.

"Awright, boys," he said and stepped back. "Take 'im away. Fr'm now on, this layout b'longs t' Logan. Don't want no fellers layin' around here an' lousin' up th' place."

Davis was dragged out of bed. When he was led out to the porch, down the steps and over to the bunkhouse, he halted momentarily, stared and swallowed hard. His eight men were lined up in front of the bunkhouse, eight sleepy-eyed, barefooted, underwear-clad men who looked up when he came nearer.

"Awright, Davis," he was told. "You're stayin' here f'r now with your men. B'have y'selves an' everything'll be awright. But if any o' you try any tricks, there'll be hell t' pay. Inside now, all o' yuh!"

Twenty-one miles away the Box-Dot ranch slept peacefully, undisturbed by any thoughts or dreams of danger. Larry Parker and his wife, Fanny, had had words after supper. Fanny, sulking, had gone off to bed in the spare room, leaving Larry to enjoy his own company in their huge double bed that Fanny's father had brought from Ohio some twenty years before. In the single bed in the spare room, Fanny turned and tossed in her unhappy sleep. Across the hall Larry, who had dozed off muttering to himself, threshed about from side to side. Finally he awoke and sat up. He heard a light footstep in the hallway and smiled. It was Fanny, he told himself smugly, returning to his side. For a moment he debated his course. He was tempted to cover himself again and feign sleep; he decided he was just as sorry as she was, so he got out of bed and went to the door. There was no light in the hallway and he frowned.

He smiled again when he thought he saw a shadowy movement.

"Fanny!" he hissed. "Come on, honey! I'm waitin' f'r yuh."

There was no reply, but the shadowy movement became an actuality. It came toward him, and Larry reached out to take Fanny's hand and guide her through the darkness. A clubbed gun swung upward and the butt came down hard, thudding against Larry's unsuspecting and unprotected head, and the rancher went down limply. Fanny Parker awoke. For a moment she lay still. Presently a smile appeared at the corners of her mouth and deepened, reflecting her happiness.

"It's Larry," she whispered to herself. She had known it at once. "I knew he'd feel bad afterwards. I'll punish him, though. I'll pretend I'm still angry with him and when he comes in, I won't even speak to him—that is, for a while, anyway."

She laughed softly and moved away from the middle of the bed. Fixing her eyes on the door, she waited for it to open. Several minutes passed but Larry did not appear. Fanny's smile vanished; in its place appeared a frown of annoyance.

"Men!" she muttered to herself. "They're so stubborn even when they're wrong, and heaven only knows when they aren't. If he thinks I'm going to get up out of this warm bed and humble myself, he's got another thought coming."

She turned over on her side and closed her eyes. But in another minute she opened them again, pushed the covers off and sat up.

"Stubborn mule!" she said half aloud. "Oh, I could shake him!"

She swung her legs over the side of the bed and probed beneath it with her bare feet until she found her slippers. Larry had made them for her of leather and wool, fashioning them like Indians' moccasins. She slipped her feet into them—the wool was warm and comforting—and stood up. She made her way to the door and listened there for a moment. She could hear nothing, and it made her even more annoyed with him than before. She opened the door as noiselessly as she could and peered out. The darkness in the hallway frightened her and she withdrew her head hastily. She was motionless for a minute; then she opened the door again. This time she stepped outside briskly, wheeled and went directly to the bedroom. She reached for the doorknob and was surprised to find the door ajar. She pushed it open wider and promptly stumbled over Larry's crumpled form. She screamed and scrambled to her feet.

"Larry!" she cried, but there was no response.

She backed away, inching herself along the wall. When she reached the door of the spare room, she whirled, burst inside and closed the door behind her. She was badly frightened now. She put her hand to her mouth to stifle a scream that arose in her tightened throat. She made her way across the room to the bureau. There was a lamp atop its broad surface. She fumbled around for a moment, frantically seeking a match. She found one and struck it; if Larry had done that, striking it on the furniture, she would have had plenty to say about it. The match flamed into light; then the wick in the lamp blazed into yellowish light. She caught up the lamp, carried it to the door, opened it cautiously and peered out. There was no sound in the hallway, no movement, nothing but a hushed silence and the pounding of a frightened woman's heart. Presently lamplight filled the hallway. Fanny's widened eyes turned toward the bedroom and the crumpled body in the doorway.

There was a bare leg visible, and a bare foot lying directly on the threshold. She stared at it, gulped and swallowed painfully.

"Larry!" she screamed again and rushed forward. She dropped to her knees beside her husband and sobbed hysterically. "Larry!"

She stiffened when she thought she heard a booted foot on the porch steps. She got to her feet quickly, whirled into the bedroom and flung open the closet door. When she came away from it, there was a rifle gripped in her free right hand. Quickly she put down the lamp, backed against the wall and waited. She could hear nothing, nothing but the thumping of her own heart, and it threatened to burst her eardrums. She stepped past her husband and into the hallway. Faint yellow light from the lamp backgrounded her and furnished light the length of the hallway and to the front door. Silently, on cushioned feet, she inched her way forward, hugging the hall wall, the rifle raised and leveled. She reached the front door, listened there for a moment, then pushed it open gently. Silvery moonlight gleamed overhead. Then she stiffened again. Thirty feet from the house were two men, and as she eyed them, they started toward the house. The rifle snapped upward and roared thunderously. One of the men staggered, turned slowly and went down on his hands and knees. His companion halted and stared at him. He whirled suddenly and his right hand streaked toward his holster. He jerked out his gun. Moonlight ran along the polished barrel.

He caught a blurred glimpse of a slim figure standing in the doorway of the house. The rifle cracked again and the Colt leaped upward and belched an angry answer. Fanny Parker sighed aloud. Her hands were suddenly and strangely numbed and the rifle, sliding out of her grip, clattered to the porch floor. She tottered and a sob broke from her lips. She sagged brokenly and fell against the door. It swung inward, carrying her along, and she fell in the hallway on her hands and knees.

"Larry!" she gasped. "Larry—please!"

A night-shirted figure emerged from the bedroom and stumbled along the hallway, halted beside her and stared down at her through dazed eyes. Fanny sighed again. Quietly she slid forward on the floor. Larry Parker turned slowly. What he had seen had failed to register on his numbed brain. He reached the front door and swayed unsteadily in the doorway. His eyes began to clear; so did his head. He saw the man on the ground and the man standing beside him; then he spied the rifle that Fanny had dropped. He caught it up and raised it. He fired, and the man dropped his gun, spun and crashed over sideways. The man whom Fanny had shot stirred and raised his head; his right arm moved. Larry turned slowly in the doorway. A Colt thundered deafeningly and Larry fell against the door. He dropped the rifle. Curiously, now his eyes went down again to Fanny and he recognized her huddled form at once.

"Fanny," he whispered.

He moved away from the door, fell against the wall and braced himself with a tremendous effort that left him panting. He smiled, groped brokenly toward his wife and fell to his knees beside her. His arm went around her.

"Fanny," he whispered again. There was no answer from her, no movement, but he did not notice it. "I'm sorry, honey. I sure wish I hadn'ta said what I did t' you t'night."

His arm fell away from her. Slowly he stiffened; then a shudder seemed to run through his body. He pitched forward on the floor. For a moment he lay still, motionless, then stirred and dragged himself to where his wife lay. Presently he was quiet again. Larry and Fanny Parker were together again, sleeping beside one another as they had done for so many years. There would never be another quarrel; never again would either of them utter a harsh word to the other. They were dead.

Old Pete Lansing came out of his house and sat down on the stone step in front of the door. Pete had found it impossible to sleep. He had slipped on his pants, donned his boots and gone outside for a breath of cool air. He glanced skyward; it was a beautiful night with a sky full of silvery moon and twinkling stars. He breathed deeply and sighed contentedly. He raised his head when he heard a stirring in the barn some fifty feet from the house.

"Reckon I ain't th' on'y one that can't sleep t'night," he muttered. "Mebbe it wasn't meant f'r a body t' sleep on a night like this. Sure is just about th' nicest night I've knowed or seen in one heck uva long time."

He sat in silence for about half an hour. Finally his head came down and his tired eyes closed gently. The metallic clatter of a horse's hoof on stone or shale rang out sharply and the old man's head jerked upward. He sat upright now, his quick eyes probing the night light. He got to his feet.

"Now what'n thunder d'you s'ppose that was?" he muttered. "Coulda swore I heard a hoof. Don't hear a danged thing now."

He listened intently for a moment. When he heard something again, he moved with surprising speed, opened the door quickly and thrust his hand inside. When he withdrew it, there was a rifle clutched tightly in it. Now there was a recognizable though distant drum of hoofs. He nodded to himself.

"Uh-huh," he muttered. "Knew I wasn't just dreamin'. Comin' closer, too."

The pounding of hoofs swelled, then suddenly died out. Pete frowned. He waited patiently, raised the rifle half a dozen times and lowered it just as often. The minutes passed slowly, five, ten, fifteen minutes. Suddenly there was a shrill whinny from the direction of the barn.

"Why, doggone it!" Pete sputtered. "So that's their game, eh? Aimin' t' run off my horses!"

He wheeled and rushed off toward the barn. He was twenty feet away when a man suddenly appeared in the moonlight. Pete jerked to an abrupt stop. The man was pulling on something—something that was definitely reluctant to be pulled out of the barn. The man cursed aloud and his voice carried over the intervening space. He lashed out with his booted foot, and a horse cried out protestingly.

"Damn you!" Pete yelled. "I'll learn you t' kick one o' my horses!"

His rifle jumped and crashed. The man turned toward him, stumbled away from the barn, stopped momentarily, then toppled over. Pete yelled again and rushed forward. He was within a dozen feet of the barn when another man came around the building. This man stopped when he saw Pete thundering toward him. It was too late for Pete to halt his headlong rush, too late for him to shoot. The man fired from the hip and Pete cried out, dropped his rifle, stumbled awkwardly and fell. The Colt flamed again, twice, three times, and Pete threshed around helplessly as he was blasted to death.

A few minutes later, nine horses were led out of the barn. Mounted men rode up, caught up the guide ropes that were tossed to them, and clattered away into the night.

Now the twinkling stars seemed to fade out. The bright, silvery moon slipped away behind a billowy, mountainous cloud that appeared out of nowhere. The earth was hushed and silent. The cool breeze rustled the grass and droned over the outstretched figure of a dead man. Then it raced away and everything was still. Darkness draped its mantle over everything, hiding the dead, hushing the lingering echoes of gunfire.

9. Canavan's Return ★

JOHNNY CANAVAN stood in the doorway of Henry Comerford's office. As usual, his thumbs were hooked in his gun belt. There was a deepening frown on his face, evidence that he was giving a lot of thought to a most annoying and distasteful subject. His horse, tied up at the rail a dozen feet from the door, turned his head and eyed him questioningly. Three men sauntered past and glanced briefly at Canavan, whose thoughts were elsewhere. They looked at the horse, then at one another.

"H'm," said one man, halting. His companions stopped, too. "Sure looks like th' feller who owns this here horse don't know th' law."

"Or mebbe he thinks Quarles is just kiddin'," another man ventured. "What d'we do 'bout it, Charlie?"

"Ain't but one thing we can do," the first man replied. "Untie 'im, Buck."

Buck, a tall, lanky man with a week's growth of beard, grinned.

"Sure," he said.

He stepped to the rail and reached for the looped reins. The horse neighed shrilly and backed away in alarm. Buck scowled darkly, vaulted the rail and grabbed the reins.

"C'mere!" he said gruffly.

The horse reared up and lashed out with ironshod

hoofs. Buck backed off hastily. When he saw his opportunity, he dashed in and whacked the animal across the rump, a pistol-like slap that echoed the length of the street. The man named Charlie and the man standing beside him were suddenly hurled apart and sent spinning. A steely hand caught Buck by the shoulder, whirled him around and sent him crashing against the rail. Buck was dazed momentarily. He came bounding off the rail and plunged blindly toward his assailant, who side-stepped nimbly, pivoted and swung hard. A big fist exploded in Buck's face, and his knees buckled beneath him. Canavan struck him a second time, and Buck collided with the rail again. Blood spouted from his nose and mouth, staining his shirt front. He sagged brokenly, slid away from the rail and toppled over in a limp heap.

Charlie had jerked out his gun. His companion, considerably more shaken up and dazed, seemed unable to do more than stare at the awkwardly outstretched Buck. Charlie's gun snapped upward. Canavan's horse wheeled suddenly, lashed out at him with his forehoofs and struck Charlie's right arm as he fired. The bullet, deflected, whined skyward. Charlie grabbed his bruised arm with his left hand.

"Drop it," Canavan said coldly. Charlie looked up to find the muzzle of Canavan's Colt gaping at him. "Drop y' gun, I said!"

Charlie frowned. He dropped his gun reluctantly and eyed it lying at his feet. His companion came to life at that moment and straightened up.

"You," Canavan said curtly, and the man seemed to wince. "Reach!"

The man raised his hands without delay. Canavan came forward, turned Buck over on his back with a prodding boot toe, bent down swiftly and jerked the man's gun out of his holster, shoving the weapon into his own belt. He came around the rail, pushed Charlie away roughly and scooped up the latter's gun.

"Looks like things've been happenin' 'round here," a voice that Canavan quickly recognized as Quarles's said behind him. Canavan turned his head, "H'llo, Red."

Canavan eyed him.

"Reckon these polecats are part o' your outfit," Canavan said. "Ain't they?"

Quarles smiled, though his eyes belied his smile.

"That's right," he replied.

"You oughta teach 'em that it ain't exactly p'lite t' go

66

'round manhandlin' other people's horses. They're li'ble t' get their teeth kicked out."

Quarles glanced at the still unconscious Buck.

"Looks t' me like you did a pretty good job on him," he said.

Canavan did not turn his head.

"I'll do a better one if he don't learn t' keep his hands where they b'long."

"Red, I'm afraid you've kinda overlooked one thing 'bout Buck an' 'is partners."

"I have? What's that?"

"If you'll kinda look at th'm a little closer, you'll find that all three o' th'm are wearin' deputies' badges."

Canavan's lip curled scornfully.

"All th' badges in th' world wouldn't help make th'm smell any better'n they do right now," he said coldly. "They'd be skunks no matter how many badges you pinned on th'm. But what's that deputy business gotta do with th'm trying' t' run off my horse?"

"They were just doin' their duty."

"Say that again."

"Th' law says nob'dy c'n leave a horse idlin' in th' street," Quarles explained patiently.

"You don't say!"

"That's th' law awright."

"I see. An' who cooked it up? You, eh?"

"Yeah, I s'ppose I had somethin' t' do with it."

"I'll bet," Canavan said. "Y'know, Quarles, I got 'n idea you're gonna run outa deputies."

"Oh, I dunno."

" 'Less you make a change in that law o' yourn," Canavan concluded.

Their eyes clashed.

"Red," Quarles said with a strange heaviness in his voice, "Red, I've allus liked you, even though you took a runout on me an' voted f'r John Richards 'stead o' stringin' along with me like you agreed."

"I'da voted f'r you awright if I hadn'ta found out a few things about you an' what you were cookin' up," Canavan retorted.

Quarles smiled again, suddenly and fleetingly. Then he was sober-faced again.

"Just wanna give you a friendly tip," he said. "Don't crowd your luck an' don't push my hand. Savvy?"

"Y'mean that if I don't quit buttin' into your game, somethin's li'ble t' happen t' me?"

"In other words, Red, yeah."

Canavan's eyes gleamed with a steely brightness.

"Now I'm gonna give you a tip, Quarles."

"I'm listenin', Red."

"Better tell your hired hands t' steer clear o' me. They'll find that pluggin' folks like th' Parkers an' ol' Pete Lansing is one thing an' that tryin' t' give me a dose o' lead poisonin' is another."

"That all?"

"Just this much more: You're ridin' high right now but, take my word f'r it, you're gonna pay through th' nose f'r what you've a'ready done 'round here. One o' these days, mister, things'll catch up with you, an' when that time comes, you'll swing."

"Mebbe, mebbe not."

"I'm willin' t' bet on it. An' don't f'rget t' tell them polecats o' yourn what I've said. Next time I have any trouble with 'em, I'll use my gun on 'em. That's a promise."

"Awright, Red. Say, ain't that Buck's gun you got tucked away in your belt?"

"Huh? Oh, yeah. Here, this one b'longs t' that feller," Canavan replied, nodding toward Charlie. He handed the gun to Quarles, then drew Buck's and handed it over, too.

"You fellers take Buck down t' th' office," Quarles said, turning to Charlie and the man with the half-raised hands. Quarles glared at him, and the man lowered his hands quickly. He looked at Canavan again. "Be seein' you, Red."

"Oh, I'll be around, awright," Canavan answered. He holstered his gun, glanced at his horse, then trudged into the *Bugle* office and promptly collided with Henry Comerford. Canavan eyed him, frowned and hooked his thumbs in his belt. "Snoopin', eh?"

The pudgy man grinned up at him and nodded.

"Uh-huh."

"Hope you got 'n earful."

"I did, and so did Mister Quarles," Comerford said. Then he laughed softly. "I don't recall that I ever enjoyed anything quite as much. Of course, that delightful walloping you handed Buck was the high spot. It was a thoroughly workmanlike job."

Canavan's frown deepened.

"Wa—al, if it was that good, you better bear it in mind an' watch your step. I'm li'ble t' hafta give you a dose o' what Buck got 'less you mind your p's an' q's."

Comerford grinned again.

"Yes, sir!"

"That's better! Got everything loaded in th' wagons?"

"Uh-huh. Everything."

"Got them what-d'ye-call-'em things handy?"

"The posters are in a package on the table."

"Colonel ready?"

"He's been ready for hours."

Canavan rubbed his chin reflectively; Henry watched him, his eyes twinkling. Finally Canavan lowered his hand and grinned down at him.

"Reckon you've taken care o' everything."

"Thanks."

"Soon's it gets good an' dark, start rollin'."

"Right. You coming along with us?"

"On'y part o' th' way," Canavan replied. "I just wanna see that you're on your way, then I'll head back here."

"And when you've finished your job?"

"I'll join you fellers at Beth's place."

Quarles had had a restless night. It was nearly dawn when he finally fell asleep. As a result, it was much later than usual when he emerged from the "K. C." Generally he was one of the first to make his appearance. He halted in the doorway, yawned and stretched himself. He seemed surprised to find the street completely awake, frowned and forgot his tiredness when he noticed a group of his men gathered around a poster that had been nailed to the wall of a building directly opposite the "K. C." He hitched up his belt, sauntered across the street and halted on the fringe of the group.

"What's goin' on here?" he demanded.

A dozen heads turned. A path opened directly to the poster.

"What's that thing?" Quarles asked, nodding toward it. "What's it about an' who put it up there?"

"Dunno who did th' nailin' up, Boss," a man answered. "But it's sure got plenty t' say 'bout you an' about some o' us."

Quarles scowled darkly.

"Tear it down," he said curtly.

"What good'll that do?" a voice asked. "Th' damned things've been plastered on every door an' wall in town."

Quarles stepped closer. The men crowded around him.

"What's it say?" a latecomer asked from the rear of the group. "Someb'dy read it out loud, will yuh?"

A man's voice droned out the captions:

> ## QUARLES RULE A REIGN OF TERROR
>
> WANTON SLAYINGS AND JUMPING OF RANCHES
> ORDERED BY QUARLES AND COMMITTED
> BY ALLEGED DEPUTIES

"I'll be damned!" a man said angrily. "How d'you like th' gall o' that thing, huh?"

"What's th' rest uv it say?" a voice called.

"Keep your shirt on an' I'll read it. It says—"

"Louder!"

"F'r Pete's sake, will you fellers gimme a chance? It says—" The man continued:

> The cold-blooded, ruthless murders of rancher Larry Parker and Mrs. Parker, followed by the equally wanton shooting down of Logan's oldest citizen, Pete Lansing, highlighted Dan Quarles's fourth day as administrator of law and order in Logan.
>
> There can be no question as to the identity of the slayers; the names of those who were involved in the jumping of a dozen ranches are also known.
>
> We have already reported those names to the proper authorities. We reprint them below:
>
> | | |
> |---|---|
> | Dan Quarles | "Slim" Bennett |
> | Steve Hammond | Stan Pritchard |
> | "Link" Smithson | "Tex" Liscombe |
> | "Tex" Dennison | "Kansas" Marston |
> | "Chuck" O'Dea | "Preacher" Gibbs |
> | "Gibby" Mello | Shad Roe |
> | Niles Porter | Mike Grover |
>
> We suggest that you watch for this bulletin. It will appear daily.
>
> THE CITIZENS' COMMITTEE
> FOR LOGAN

"I'll be doggoned!" a man said in awed tones.

"Yeah," another man said. "Now how'n hell d'you s'ppose they got them names, huh?"

Quarles turned around. He was grim-faced and tight-lipped.

"On'y got one printer in Logan," he said coldly. "Let's go see th' polecat. Mebbe he knows somethin'."

With Quarles at the head of the group and some twenty men strung out behind him, the procession marched up the street. Other men appeared, some on the opposite side, and others who were just emerging from the hotel; they came striding over and fell in behind the marchers. Presently they halted in front of the *Bugle*. Quarles tried the door. It was locked. A couple of men peered into the place through the windows.

"Hey, Boss!" one man called excitedly. "Th' danged place is plumb empty!"

Quarles did not answer. He stepped back and hurled himself at the door. There was a tearing, splintering sound, and the door flew open, crashing against something inside. Quarles, carried along by the impetus of his rush, plunged into the place. Three or four of his men followed close behind him. The *Bugle* office was really empty except for a broken chair and a battered table that stood against a wall; when someone brushed against it, it slid away from the wall, leaving one table leg still standing. Slowly almost gently, the table upended itself and, like a sinking ship, settled itself on the floor.

"Anybody see or hear anything o' Comerford movin'?" Quarles asked over his shoulder.

"There wasn't anything outa th' way 'round here when I come by, yesterd'y afternoon," a man said in reply. "Hey, Spud, you were with me."

"That's right," the man named Spud said with a nod. "Matter o' fact, now that I think uv it, them danged presses were hammerin' away like all get out."

"Hammerin' out them damned posters," Quarles said grimly. "I wish I'da knowed what was goin' on in here, b'lieve me!"

A man came striding into the store. He shouldered his way through to Quarles.

"Boss," he said quickly. Quarles turned. "There's wagon tracks outside 'round th' back leading away t' th' north. Reckon that's th' answer t' what b'come o' Mister Comerford."

"Oh, yeah?"

"But what'd he head north f'r?" a man demanded. "There's nothing northw'rd f'r mebbe two hundred miles, leastways till yuh get through th' hill country an' break out into th' open again. What's more, th' danged fool oughta know no wagon's gonna make it through them hills."

"Mebbe he don't know," another man said.

"He knows a heap more'n any o' you figger," Quarles said sharply. "You fellers keep yammerin' away 'bout him headin' northw'rd, an' I'll bet you anything y'like he didn't go northw'rd a-tall."

"Huh? What d'you mean, Boss?"

"Y' mean them tracks ain't real?"

"Aw, use your heads," Quarles said impatiently. " 'Course them tracks are real. Nob'dy c'n fake wagon tracks. You all oughta know that well's I do. But what none o' you seem t' understand is that them tracks are just a cover-up."

"I don't get it, Boss."

"Doggone it, Curly," Quarles exploded, "you're even dumber 'n you look! Figger it out this way: Comerford was hitailin', so since he didn't wanna be seen, he couldn't just drive 'is wagon down th' street where everybody would see 'im, could he?"

"N—o, reckon not."

"So he just drove away fr'm th' rear. Get it? An' t' make it look good, he headed north."

"That's what I said, Boss—northw'rd."

"Yeah, that's what everybody said!" Quarles yelled. "But he didn't go northw'rd!"

"Oh!"

"D'pend on it, soon's he felt it was safe, he swung southw'rd an' finally drove eastw'rd like he was plannin' to all along. Now d'you get it?"

"Yeah, sure," Curly said quickly. "Wa—al, what d'we do?"

"F'r one thing," Quarles said in answer, "startin' t'night, we're gonna post guards 'round th' town. We're gonna c'rral th' feller who puts up th' posters."

There was a general nodding of heads.

"That's one job I'll ask for, Boss," a man said quickly. "I'd sure like t' get my hands on that feller, no matter who he is."

"Who else could it be but Comerford?" Curly asked. "That is, if he's th' one who done th' printin' o' them danged posters."

Quarles turned slowly. Curly colored.

"Why'n hell don't you shut up?" Quarles demanded. "You don't know fr'm nuthin', but that don't keep you fr'm yammerin' all th' time. Mebbe if you listened f'r a spell 'stead o' allus doin' th' talkin', you might learn somethin'."

"Aw, Boss—"

"Shut up!" Quarles roared. There was a moment's silence, then he turned to the other men. " 'Course it wasn't Comerford who put up them damned things. Anybody with on'y half a brain'd know that much. Comerford ain't got th' guts f'r anything but printin'. It was another feller, an' f'r my dough it wasn't anybody but Canavan."

"Doggone it, Boss, I think you've got somethin' there!" a man said quickly. "Don't you fellers savvy that?"

"Yeah," another man said, " 'course I do."

"On'y way t' figger it," a third man added.

"Thanks," Quarles said dryly. "One o' you fellers go round up Buck Peterson, Charlie Thomas an' that Dave Wills. Tell th'm I got a job f'r th'm t' do."

Curly headed for the door.

"Wait a minute," Quarles called, and Curly halted and looked back over his shoulder. Quarles smiled coldly. "Tell th'm th' job's got somethin' t' do with Red Canavan. They'll come a-hustlin' then."

10. Trick for Trick ★

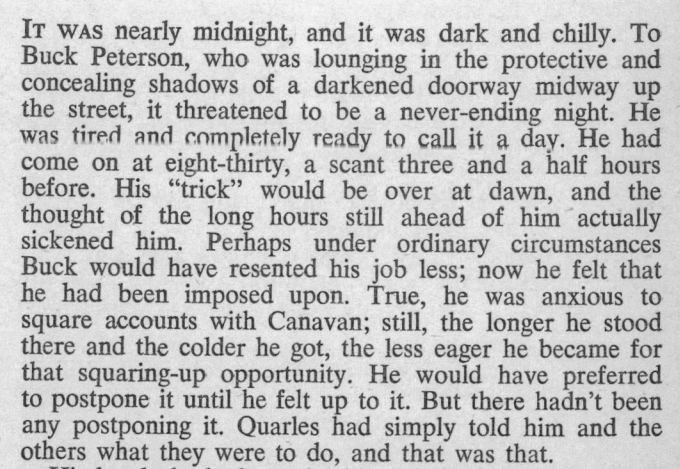

IT WAS nearly midnight, and it was dark and chilly. To Buck Peterson, who was lounging in the protective and concealing shadows of a darkened doorway midway up the street, it threatened to be a never-ending night. He was tired and completely ready to call it a day. He had come on at eight-thirty, a scant three and a half hours before. His "trick" would be over at dawn, and the thought of the long hours still ahead of him actually sickened him. Perhaps under ordinary circumstances Buck would have resented his job less; now he felt that he had been imposed upon. True, he was anxious to square accounts with Canavan; still, the longer he stood there and the colder he got, the less eager he became for that squaring-up opportunity. He would have preferred to postpone it until he felt up to it. But there hadn't been any postponing it. Quarles had simply told him and the others what they were to do, and that was that.

His headache had eased a bit and the furious trip-hammering in his ears had dwindled to a faint buzzing. However, the chill night air bothered his battered nose and bruised mouth to an irritating degree. He glanced toward the "K. C.," and his frown deepened. Quarles and many of the others were in the "K. C." and doubtless they were idling away their time in warmth and comfort, while he—well, the thought rankled within him. He turned his head and studied a shadow in a doorway some twenty feet beyond him. When the shadow moved, Buck grunted. That was Charlie Thomas's post. Buck peered out cautiously. The street was deserted and the "K. C." was the only establishment that still showed a light. He whistled and Charlie stepped out of his place of concealment and looked toward him. Buck motioned to him, and Charlie, a bit hesitant at first, finally came striding up the street, hugging the front of the darkened buildings to avoid detection. Presently Charlie came up to him.

"S' matter?" Charlie asked.

"Aw, everything," Buck grumbled. "How'n hell does Quarles know Canavan's comin' back t'night?"

"Poster says it's gonna be changed daily," Thomas replied. "Hey, it's doggoned cold, ain't it?"

"It's colder'n hell," Buck said, "an' I feel lousy. I got a buzzin' in my head an' ears like there was bees in it. An' that damned cold air makes me wanna blow m' nose an', doggone it, I'm a-scared to."

"You seen anything o' Dave?"

"He's up th' street a ways," Buck answered. "I sure wish I was in bed, or even in th' 'K. C.' right now. I'd give most anything f'r a drink."

"I could do with one, too," Charlie said with a grin. His white, even teeth flashed in the night light.

"Wa—al?" Buck demanded.

"Wa—al, what?"

"Why don't we go do somethin' about it?"

Charlie shrugged his shoulders.

"Oh, I dunno. 'Course Quarles'll raise holy hell but, heck, he ain't freezin' 'is ears off out here like we are."

"That's just it," Buck said quickly. He hitched up his belt. "Come on."

Together they trudged down the street. Dave Willis, scanning the street from his post, watched them for a moment and saw them go into the "K. C."

"How d'you like that?" he muttered. "They c'n go in an' get warmed up. Me, I gotta stay put out here an' freeze. Wa—al, they ain't no better'n me, so I'm gonna get me somethin' warm, too. Th' hell with this!"

Dave emerged from his doorway post, hitched up his pants and started down the street. He came abreast of an alley. Steely hands grabbed him and choked him into silence. When he struggled anew and sought to cry out, a fist thudded against his jaw and Dave collapsed in his captor's arms. Dave was quickly dragged down the alley. He was gagged with his own handkerchief, and his arms were bound behind him. Then he was hoisted into the saddle of a waiting horse and finally lashed to the animal.

It was probably twenty minutes later when Buck Peterson and Charlie Thomas, warmed and cheered inwardly, came out of the "K. C." They trudged up the street. When they came to Charlie's post, they halted briefly.

"Wa—al," Charlie said with a grin, "reckon this is where I get off. See you later."

"You betcha," Buck answered. He patted the bulge in his jacket pocket. "I better go give Dave a swallow o' this b'fore he freezes t' death."

"Tell 'im t' have one on me," Charlie said.

He stepped into the shadowy doorway. Buck cut across the street. Charlie watched him for a moment, then turned away, whipped up his coat collar, buttoned it around his neck and squatted down in a corner of the doorway. Buck swung close to the buildings. When he came abreast of the alley into which Dave had disappeared, he stopped, took a bottle from his pocket, uncorked it, tilted it and swallowed a mouthful.

"A—a—ah!" he muttered and smacked his lips.

The muzzle of a gun was suddenly jammed into his ribs and Buck stiffened. A hand came around his waist and jerked his gun out of his holster; the hand made a second trip around him and took the bottle out of his hands.

"Awright," a voice hissed in his ear. "Back up."

Buck hesitated. The muzzle of the gun prodded him, and Buck backed up as directed.

"Put your hands b'hind you."

Buck obeyed. There was a great, rising fear in his heart. He expected the gun in his captor's hand to come crashing down on his head, and he winced in anticipation. His wrists were swiftly and expertly bound together, then he was swung around. A gag was shoved into his mouth, and the suddenness with which his jaws were pried open made his nose hurt; he winced a second time, this time aloud. He was led down the alley; it was dark and he could see little. He stopped abruptly when a horse suddenly loomed up directly in front of him.

"Awright," the voice behind him said curtly. "Climb up."

His left foot was jerked from under him. Buck nearly fell; his captor caught him, steadied him and got Buck's foot into a stirrup; then he was fairly hoisted into the saddle. He fell forward and collided with the body of another man already seated in the saddle. Buck pulled back hastily and managed to straighten himself up. For a moment he felt a great uneasiness; then, strangely, he felt better. The fact that he had been taken prisoner bothered him only briefly; that he hadn't been hit over the head was the all-important thing, and he relaxed. He turned his head slightly, wondering whether his captor was still beside him; he looked down. There was no immediate sign of the man. He decided to look no further. Perhaps if he gave no trouble, nothing much would happen to him. He wondered about the man in front of him and eyed him for a moment. Presently he closed his eyes.

Charlie Thomas got to his feet and dug into his pockets.
"Aw, hell!" he muttered in disgust.
Then he recalled that Buck had asked him for a cigarette and that he had given his makings to him at the "K. C." bar.

He stepped out of the doorway and started up the street. He glanced at Buck's post as he came abreast of it, crossed the street as he had seen Buck do and reached the alley. Mechanically he turned his head. He thought he heard something in the alley and he stopped.

"Buck," he called softly, "that you in there?"

He heard an answering "Uh-huh" and turning into the alley, started down its darkened length. He whirled when he heard a quick step behind him, but it was too late. A gun butt crashed against his head and he grunted and fell like a poled steer. He caromed off a wall, struck on his shoulder and rolled over. A shadowy figure quickly bent over him.

Dan Quarles awoke early the next morning. He dressed and came striding out of the "K. C." The street was deserted and he nodded approvingly. His eyes turned toward the poster on the building wall directly opposite the "K. C." He stared at it for a moment, turned his head away, then jerked his head around again. He plunged across the street, stopped and looked up at the poster. A single glance told him that it had happened; this was the promised poster, a new one. He stared at it incredulously. His lips tightened; he whirled around and pulled out his gun. It thundered deafeningly in the dawn air.

"Buck!" he roared. "Charlie! Dave!"

The slow-fading echo of gunfire lingered in the air, blending with the echo of his voice. But there was no reply from any of the three guards. A window in the hotel was flung open, and a head with a tousled mop of unruly hair and a face with sleepy, squinting eyes appeared.

"Hey, you!" the awakened man yelled. "What th' hell's th' idea, huh?"

Quarles's eyes blazed. His gun snapped upward; it roared, and the windowpane directly above the man's head fell in with a shattering crash, showering him with bits of broken glass. Hastily he withdrew his head. Now men came pouring into the street, sleepy-eyed, half-dressed men, many with guns gripped in their hands.

"C'mere!" Quarles yelled.

Most of the men stared at him for an awakening moment; a few of them, more alert than the others, recognized him at once and came pounding to his side. The rest followed at their heels.

"Look!" Quarles yelled, pointing a shaking finger at the poster. "Look at that!"

Men crowded around him, barefooted and booted men with the latter treading on the former.

"Y'know," one man said, " 'less I'm plumb locoed, that don't look like th' same thing that was up there yest'd'y. Leastways, it don't look like it t' me."

Quarles whirled upon him.

" 'Course it ain't, yuh dumb ape!" he roared. "If it was, d'you think I'd be hollerin' m' head off now?"

"Oh!" the man said lamely and flushed.

"I gave Buck Peterson, Charlie Thomas an' Dave Wills th' job o' standin' guard 'round here last night," Quarles went on heatedly, "so's we could grab th' feller who put that thing up there. We knew he was comin'. Th' first sign said there was gonna be a new one every day. So what happened? That!" Quarles said, pointing again to the poster. "That's what happened!"

"Th' boys have any expl'nation f'r it?" another man asked. When Quarles turned to him, he wished he hadn't opened his mouth.

"Are you kiddin'?" Quarles demanded. "I ain't seen hide nor hair o' Buck or o' th' others since last night."

"Think anything coulda happened t' th'm?" a voice in the crowd asked.

"F'r their sake I hope a lot's happened t' th'm," Quarles said gruffly. "If they're still awright when I see th'm, they won't be afterwards."

There was a general exchange of significant glances among the men.

"You fellers spread out," Quarles said shortly. "Half o' yuh take this side o' th' street, half th' other side. I want every doorway, store an' alleyway searched. Don't pass up anything, not even a hole in th' ground. You'll find th'm aroun' somewheres, prob'ly cockeyed as all hell."

"Uh-huh," a man said, nodding. "I was in th' 'K. C.' kinda late last night an'—"

Quarles interrupted him with an impatient gesture.

"I know, I know," he said curtly. "Buck an' Charlie come in an' got th'mselves a couple o' drinks an'—"

"An' took a bottle out with th'm," the man added dryly.

"Get started," Quarles said, disregarding the man's final comment.

The men turned and plodded away. Quarles, his hands on his hips, looked up at the poster.

WESTERN EYES FOCUSED ON LOGAN

AUTHORITIES STUDYING SITUATION AS LAWLESS
ELEMENTS CONTINUE TO RUN WILD

"Huh!" Quarles muttered half aloud. His eyes shifted to the more compact body of type below the captions.

> The Quarles rule of terror continues unabated in Logan. Law enforcement officers of neighboring towns are eyeing the situation and studying it in anticipation of a spreading of the disorders. Posses and emergency rider groups are standing by, ready for instantaneous action.
>
> Officers of bordering States have submitted the names of fugitives now believed to be harbored by Quarles. These names are rapidly being

checked. Thus far the following have been confirmed:

"Giddy" Parks
    Wanted for murder in Clay County, Colorado
Dave Wills
    Wanted for armed robbery in Iron County, Colorado
Charlie Thomas
    Wanted for murder in Hawkes County, Colorado, and for armed robbery in Lee County, Colorado
"Buck" Peterson
    Wanted for murder in Wade County, California
"Slim" Bennett
    Wanted for armed robbery in Sacramento City, California
John Lippert
    Wanted for murder in Desert City, Arizona
Homer "Skipper" Jones
    Wanted for armed robbery in Tombstone, Nevada
Jack and Pete Billings
    Cousins, wanted for armed robbery in Hill County, Colorado

Larry Jacks and "Monk" Hurley, wanted for murder in Ohio and Kansas, respectively, have been found dead of gunshot wounds and as such have been stricken from the lists of wanted men.

THE CITIZENS' COMMITTEE
FOR LOGAN

Quarles, tight-lipped, turned on his heel, trudged across the street and went into the "K. C."

Sunrays filtered into the "K. C." through the dust-streaked windows, skipped lightly, fantastically, over the rows of bottles behind the bar and made curious designs on the cracked mirror behind the bottles. The place was empty save for a lone figure at the far end of the bar. It was Dan Quarles and he was thoughtfully motionless. A burly man came in and halted in the doorway. Quarles raised his head, and the man strode toward him, stopping beside him.

"When'd you get back?" Quarles asked.

Tex Murray shoved his hat back from his eyes. He leaned over the bar.

"Just now," he answered. "What'n blazes is goin' on 'round here?"

Quarles grunted.

"Nothing much. Why?"

"You seen that poster across th' street?"

"Sure. They're all over th' street."

"What d'you make uv 'em, Dan? An' what's that Citizens' C'mittee?"

"Just another name f'r ranchers. How many men did you line up?"

"Forty-eight," Murray replied. "They oughta start driftin' in in a couple o' days. Might be a dozen more'n th' forty-eight."

"Wish it was a couple o' hundred," Quarles said. "Then we'd be all set."

"This is on'y th' b'ginnin', Dan. But tell me what you got planned."

"Wa—al," Quarles began, "I've picked th' spots f'r th' new towns. We'll plant mebbe fifteen men in each spot, get 'em started puttin' up shacks, an' keep addin' t' 'em as we get more men."

"Uh-huh. What kind o' spots did you pick?"

Quarles grinned at him.

"What kind d'you think? They're all on high ground, easy t' d'fend. F'r my dough they're right where stage lines should cross. Th' idea is t' populate th' places an' make 'em grow. We're b'ginnin' with a circle an' we'll widen it as we get stronger. Logan'll be right smack in th' middle."

"That's some idea, Dan."

"It come t' me a couple o' months ago, an' I've been thinkin' about it an' buildin' it up in my mind. All I wanted was a chance t' really go t' work on it, an' now we're doin' it."

"You're takin' in cattle country—"

"Damned rich country," Quarles said, interrupting. "It's got everything, includin' water. This is gonna be somethin' lots o' men've dreamed about but never got anywheres with. I'm gonna see it come true."

"Got a name picked out f'r it?"

"Don't need any. Everybody'll know about it."

"Yeah, reckon that's right, Dan. Th' 'Kingdom o' th' Lawless,' eh?"

"That's th' gen'ral idea, Tex. An' I'm gonna be top man, an' you'll be next. We'll own everything—stores, s'loons, banks, ranches, everything. Gimme a thousan' men, an' along with others that'll drift in outa nowheres, we'll be so strong it'll take n' army, an' a damned good one, t' root us out. Call it anything y'like—a kingdom, 'n empire, anything a-tall. It'll be a new country, all by itself."

A man came striding into the café. Quarles and Murray turned when they heard his step.

"Want me, John?" Quarles asked.

The man nodded.

"Awright," Quarles said. "Come over here."

John came forward and stopped in front of him. He looked at Murray and nodded to him.

"Howdy, Sheriff. Boss," John said, turning to Quarles, "there ain't a sign o' Buck or th' others an', b'lieve me, we've covered every inch o' Logan. They just ain't aroun'."

Quarles frowned. Murray looked at him sharply.

"Huh? What's this all about?"

"I'll tell you about it later on," Quarles said in reply. "Anything else, John?"

The man nodded.

"Boss, did you know Lem Gorman was pullin' outa town?" he asked.

"Gorman?" Quarles repeated. "Th' feller who runs that gen'ral store?"

"Yeah," John said, nodding, "that's th' feller, on'y he don't run anything now. He's sold out."

"T' who?"

"T' that Canavan."

The frown on Quarles's face deepened.

"T' Canavan?" he repeated. "I don't get it."

"Wa—al, it seems like Canavan come t' see Gorman late last night, got 'im outa bed, made a deal with 'im f'r all th' groceries an' stuff Gorman had, an' took 'em away. Canavan musta had a wagon somewheres aroun' an' he made Gorman turn in again while he lugged th' stuff out th' back door. This mornin', when Gorman looked in, th' danged place was plumb empty 'cept f'r th' shelves an' th' counter."

"Hey," Murray said, "I don't like that."

"Neither do I," Quarles said. "Look, John, don't go shootin' off your mouth 'bout this. Savvy?"

"I don't know fr'm nuthin', Boss."

"As f'r that lousy Gorman," Quarles continued, "I'd like t' beat 'is damned head off."

Murray eyed him, grinning.

"Mebbe th' sheriff oughta go see Mister Gorman," he said, "an' kinda have a talk with 'im. What d'you think, Dan?"

"Nope," John said, shaking his head. "It's too late f'r that now."

"Huh?" Murray demanded. "What d'you mean?"

"Gorman's gone," John answered. "Left soon's I finished talkin' with 'im."

11. The Strength of the Weak ★

BETH RICHARDS stood in the open doorway of her kitchen. Henry Comerford and Colonel Wynn appeared and joined her.

"What's going on?" Comerford asked.

"Sh-h-h!" Beth said quickly. "Listen!"

Outside, about a dozen paces from the house, twenty men stood in a circle with Canavan in the middle of it.

"Awright, men," they heard Canavan say. "This is it. T'night we take t' th' saddle. In th' mornin' we'll chalk up another hefty wallop against Mister Quarles an' his outfit. Half o' you are ridin' under Stanton, th' other half under Carroll. They're both good men. You fellers know that even better'n I do. Anyway, they know th' job t' be done. Take your orders fr'm them. If you've got any questions t' ask, ask 'em now. We don't want anything comin' up once you're under way. Awright. Any questions?"

There was no reply. The men grinned at him and shook their heads.

"Swell," Canavan said. "Awright, Stanton, Carroll. Get goin'. An' good luck!"

The men turned and trudged away. A few minutes later the air was filled with the pounding of hoofs; horsemen clattered past, wheeled their mounts and rode off. Canavan hitched up his belt, turned and grinned when he saw Beth in the doorway.

"Very well done, General," Comerford called over her shoulder.

Canavan grinned and sauntered up to the doorway.

"Loafin' again?" he demanded of Comerford in mock severity.

"The posters were finished hours ago," the pudgy man replied. "How 'bout takin' another man with you on your little expedition?"

"You askin' again? What's th' matter? Got nothing t' do aroun' here?" Canavan demanded. "Beth, can't you dig up somethin' f'r him t' do?"

Beth smiled.

"The dishes are done and put away," she answered. "Besides, Mr. Comerford breaks too many when he wipes them. I'm afraid I'm going to have to transfer him to another department."

Canavan's eyebrows arched.

"Oh, yeah? Wa—al, got any ideas? Think he might be uv any use in th' barn? We c'n use a top hand out there t' help clean up th' mess, y'know."

"Oh, I think that would be wonderful! Think of the experience, Mr. Comerford."

There was a snort from Comerford. He turned on his heel and tramped away. Colonel Wynn followed him. Beth's eyes ranged over Canavan.

"You're off again?" she asked presently.

"Uh-huh," he said.

"Back to Logan?"

"Yep. Gotta keep Quarles posted on what's goin' on, y'know," he said lightly.

"Must—must you do it yourself?"

"Someb'dy's gotta do it. You wouldn't want me t' give someb'dy else th' job just b'cause somethin' might happen, would you?"

Beth did not answer.

"Wa—al, time f'r me t' get goin'," he said, hitched up his belt and turned. "See you later on."

He strode away toward the barn. There were half a dozen men idling near it. When he approached, they came forward to meet him.

"All set?" he asked.

"Just waitin' f'r you," a man replied.

"Tell th' boys t' get their horses so's we c'n get goin'," Canavan answered.

Beth was mounting the stairs that led to the upper floor when she heard the swelling clatter of approaching hoofs. She stopped mechanically and listened. Horsemen thundered past the house at full gallop; in another minute they were gone. The echo of their horses' pounding hoofs faded out. Slowly Beth went upstairs.

It was evening. Mother Jones's place was well crowded, as were the other two "eateries" on the street. Men at the counter in Mother's place idled over their coffee. At the tables the service was a bit slower. Presently Mother Jones, laboring under a huge tray of coffee cups, emerged from the tiny kitchen at the rear. There was a sudden roar of rifle fire. Men sat upright; some paled, while a few got to their feet. A bullet whined and struck a swinging ceiling lamp and sent it plunging to the floor, where it seemed to disintegrate with an explosive crash. Men whirled past Mother Jones. The tray flew out of her hands when she was bumped. Steaming coffee drenched her and spattered the counter and wall while men dove under tables. Mother Jones screamed, wheeled and fled into the kitchen. Along the street the rolling thunder of rifle fire smashed windows, adding to the din.

A lead slug shattered a window in the "K. C.," and the men at the bar abandoned it hastily. The bullet plowed into a row of bottles, smashed them and spewed liquor over the startled bartender. He gulped, turned and dashed to the rear. Men, stumbling over one another, rushed pell-mell toward the side wall, dropped to their knees there and waited for another flare-up of gunfire.

Dan Quarles and Tex Murray had finished their supper. They were sitting in the latter's office, their feet hoisted atop the desk. A bullet splintered the wooden panel in the upper part of the door and sent the two men skittering out of their chairs to the floor. They dove for the desk and huddled behind it. They turned as one. The bullet had spent itself and buried itself in the wall directly behind the desk.

"Whew!" Murray said. "That was kinda close, wasn't it?"

"When they come that close," Quarles said grimly, "they ain't no accident. Let's go have a look outside."

"Wait a minute," Murray cautioned.

They huddled on their knees for a minute, but there was no new outburst of gunfire. They got to their feet. Quarles jerked out his gun and trudged to the door. Murray came up behind him. Quarles gripped the knob, turned it, opened the door and peered out.

"See anything?" Murray asked at his elbow.

Quarles shook his head.

"Nope," he answered, "not a damned thing."

The street was now oppressively hushed. In the air was the faint, lingering echo of gunfire.

"Come on," Quarles said over his shoulder.

Murray drew his gun and followed him into the street. They looked toward the "K. C." and saw men pouring out. Murray caught Quarles's arm.

"Look!" he said quickly.

"Huh? Where?"

"On th' wall," Murray said. "Right near th' door."

They stared hard.

"Th' nerve o' that galoot," Murray muttered, "nailin' that thing up there, right under our noses!"

"So that's what all th' shootin' was about!" Quarles said. "It was a cover-up f'r th'm while th' signs were bein' put up."

Murray said nothing. He was reading the captions on the poster.

WESTERN LAW IN ACTION

AUTHORITIES MOVE TO WIPE OUT QUARLES GANG

"Oh, yeah?" Quarles said gruffly. "Let's see what they c'n do, damn 'em!"

> Law enforcement officers from bordering States have aligned themselves with local authorities and the result is a move to wipe out the Dan Quarles organization now running rampant in Logan.
>
> In two lightning strokes, ranches overrun by units of Quarles's outfit were retaken and the intruders killed or captured. The names of "Slim" Bennett, Hoagie Clemens, Rufe Taylor, Ed Peace, Eli Simms and Ed Lovett were removed from the wanted list. Among those taken prisoner and turned over to warrant-bearing officers were:
>
> | | | |
> |---|---|---|
> | Gabe Francis | Milo Dancer | Sven Kull |
> | Lorimer Paul | Pete Walker | Mike Danko |
> | Joe Westly | Leo Lawton | Lee Gibson |
>
> Warning is hereby given to all others who have

> taken refuge under Dan Quarles' protective organization that the law will never cease in its search for wanted criminals.
>
> CITIZENS' COMMITTEE
FOR LOGAN

"H'm!" Murray said. "Danko an' Kull captured an' 'Slim' Bennett killed! Dan, this kind o' thing can't go on. 'Less we c'n put a stop to it, we're done f'r. First thing y'know, they'll be closin' in on us."

"Don't be a fool!" Quarles snapped. "They talk a heap bigger'n they do. S'pose they have knocked off ten or even twenty o' our men—so what? We got a couple o' times that many on their way here, ain't we?"

"Yeah," Murray said, brightening. "That's right."

"F'r every one o' ours they get, we'll get two new ones t' take 'is place."

"Uh-huh," Murray said. "But ain't there anything we c'n do now t' kinda let 'em know we ain't asleep—some way o' joltin' 'em into knowin' we're still aroun'? This sittin' aroun' on our fannies ain't no good f'r any uv us, Dan. Th' men are gonna get restless, mebbe outa hand, 'less we get 'em movin' an' doin'. Just lettin' 'em sit aroun' while their pals are gettin' shot down an' others grabbed off by th' law—wa—al, that can't lead t' anything good."

"We'll get goin' again startin' t'morrow night."

Murray looked up quickly, interestedly.

"Oh, yeah?"

Quarles nodded.

"I'm sendin' out a big bunch o' th' boys," he went on, "An' this time, when we strike, it'll be f'r keeps. 'Course we can't send 'em out all at one time. If Canavan an' that danged citizens' c'mmittee is keepin' 'n eye on Logan, that'd on'y tip 'em off that somethin' big is cookin'. 'Stead, we'll send 'em out in small bunches an' they'll ride off in diff'rent d'rections. Get th' idea?"

"Yeah, sure," Murray answered, "an' it's a smart idea."

" 'Course," Quarles added, "they'll meet later on under cover o' darkness, an' once they get goin', there ain't anything or anybody that c'n stop 'em. We're on our way t' big things an' I don't aim t' have anybody gum up th' works."

Some miles away, five horsemen sat astride their mounts in the shadows of a bouldered incline. They were silent and thoughtful; there was no movement among them save an occasional glance at the dark sky. A horse whinnied softly and the five men sat upright in their saddles. There was a muffled hoofbeat; it swelled a bit, and presently a sixth horseman rode up and checked his mount when he spotted the shadowy figures.

"Tommy?" he called.

"Yeah, Tex," one of the men answered. "Come ahead."

The newcomer spurred his horse, loped up, reined in and swung his mount around.

"Got here soon's I could," Tex said. He eyed the men. "Don't think I know your friends, Tommy."

The latter's answer was a youthful laugh.

" 'Course y'do, Tex. Mebbe th' darkness makes 'em look diff'rent, but that feller nearest you is Joe Hicks. That's Pete Waters 'longside o' Joe."

Tex Murray laughed softly.

"Hell," he said, laughing again, "in th' darkness they look like ranchers. How are yuh, boys?"

"Mebbe you don't reco'nize th' others, Tex, but them two kinda hangin' back are th' McDowells, Jess an' Paddy."

"Oh, sure!" Murray said. "Now that I know who they are, 'course I reco'nize 'em. What's this all about, Tom?"

"Wa—al," the latter began, "it's this way, Tex: we wanna know somethin'."

"Awright. What is it that's botherin' you?"

"Tex, you're Quarles's right-hand man. B'sides, you're my brother. What's cookin'?"

"D'pends on what you mean."

"Hell, Tom," Hicks said, a bit impatiently, "cut ou th' beatin' aroun' th' bush an' come t' th' point, will yuh? It's gettin' later every minute, y'know, an' if we're pullin' out, let's get goin' while th' goin's still good."

"Pullin' out?" Tex echoed in surprise.

"Uh-huh," Tom said, a bit more briskly than before. "We don't like this here set-up under Quarles. All we c'n see, leastways all we've been able t' see up t' now, Tex, is that lots o' our friends are gettin' plugged or caught an' handed over t' th' law an' nuthin's bein' done about it."

"Go on," Tex commanded quietly.

" 'Course we'll set tight an' string along with Dan f'r a while longer if you say th' word, Tex. You brought us out here an' we know you'll give us th' right steer. But if all we c'n look for'ard to is a hangin' party, we're hittin' th' trail, an' pronto. What d'you say?"

"I'm gonna hafta answer you this way," Tex said slowly. " 'Course I know what Quarles is workin' on, an' f'r my dough it's gonna be swell. Mebbe it'll be swell f'r you fellers, too. But that's all I c'n tell you now, Tom."

"An' that ain't such a helluva lot, is it?" Hicks said.

"Nope," Tex answered calmly, "it ain't."

"Wa—al, Tom?" Hicks asked, turning to him.

"Wait a minute," Tex said. "There's another way o' lookin' at this thing, an' b'fore any o' you d'cide one way or another, take a look at it fr'm this angle."

"Go ahead," Tom said. "We're listenin'."

"Wa—al," Tex began, "let's cut out th' kiddin' an' fencin' aroun' an' look at th' facts."

"Now you're talkin'," Hicks said.

"You fellers are wanted by th' law same's everybody else in Logan," Tex continued. "Your names ain't showed up yet on them danged posters, but they will sooner or later an' you know it."

"What's th' point?" Hicks demanded. "I don't get it."

"I ain't finished yet," Tex said somewhat curtly. "If we get snowed under—an' I don't figger that c'n happen nohow—we'll all swing. If you hitail it, you'll be on your own with nob'dy t' turn to. If you run into a posse—an' you c'n bet your last buck on it th' law's keepin' 'n eye on goin's an' comin's in Logan—you'll swing. So it's a chance you're takin' any way you look at it, an' f'r my dough I'll stick t' Quarles till I know I'm doin' th' wrong thing."

"There y'are," Tom Murray said. "I tol' you fellers Tex knows all th' answers an' that he'd tell us what's what an' what t' do. Didn't I?"

"He ain't tol' us anything yet," Hicks said coldly. "Mebbe it's worth while f'r him t' string along with Quarles. He's got lots t' gain. I don't see it that way f'r us nohow. What's more, I don't aim t' set still an' wait f'r some feller t' come along an' loop a rope aroun' my neck an' me do nuthin' about it. I'm willin' t' take a chance on bein' run down by a posse. At least I won't swing. If I hafta die, I'll go out with m' gun blazin', an' that's a heap better break'n we c'n expect t' get if we stay holed up in Logan. I'm ridin'!"

He wheeled his horse, halted him momentarily and looked back over his shoulder.

"You fellers stayin', or comin' with me?" he called. "Jess? Paddy?"

Pete Waters had offered no opinion throughout the conversation. Now he sat upright in his saddle and tightened his grip on the reins.

"I'm trailin' along with Joe," he announced. He wheeled his horse, guided him past Tex's mount and pulled up alongside Hicks's.

"Reckon there ain't much choice f'r us," Jess McDowell said. "Come on, Paddy."

The brothers rode forward and joined Hicks and Waters.

"Wa—al, Tom?" Hicks called. "What'll it be?"

Tom and Tex looked at each other for a moment. Then the youth thrust out his right hand.

"So long, Tex," he said.

"So long, Kid."

They gripped hands. Hicks, Waters and the McDowells rode away into the night.

"They're my pals," Tom said awkwardly; then, a bit gently, "You understan', don't you?"

"Sure. But you kinda watch your step, y'hear?"

Tom Murray laughed lightly, boyishly.

"Don't I allus?" he said.

They parted. Tom spurred his horse and dashed away in pursuit of his friends. Tex wheeled his mount slowly and rode back to Logan.

Miles away, eastward, shadowy figures squatted on the grass atop a rise in the range. They were five in number. Now a sixth man with his rifle slung over his shoulder came toward them.

"Comp'ny's comin'," he announced and dropped down in the grass.

There was no reply. The other men were listening.

"I c'n hear 'em now," one man said presently.

"You know what t' do," the first man said in a matter-of-fact tone.

"Sure."

"Just let 'em ride up till they get 'bout halfway, then let 'em have it."

There was no need for further instructions. The men spread out, sprawled out in the grass, their rifles readied. The echoing roll of horses' hoofs on the cushioning, grassy ground grew louder, then a galloping horseman loomed up. He pulled up, wheeled and waited for his companions to catch up with him. Then he spurred his mount and sent him racing up the incline with the others strung out behind him. They reached the halfway mark, when the six rifles roared as one, an earsplitting, maddening thunder of rifle fire. Horses screamed in pain and terror; two of them reared up on their hind legs and crashed over backwards, pinning their riders beneath them.

Pete Waters, bullet-blasted, was wafted out of his saddle. He was dead before he landed in a broken heap on the ground. Jess and Paddy McDowell died within an arm's reach of each other, crushed beneath the weight of their horses. Caught within a deadly cross fire that swept everything before it, Tom Murray was bullet-riddled. He fell forward in the saddle; his mount wheeled, jogged down the incline and trotted away with him.

It remained for Joe Hicks to carry the bloodied banners for which his companions had died. Thrown by his horse when the first fusillade smashed the animal's legs and sent him plunging to the ground, Joe managed to get to his feet. Gun in hand, he struggled up the incline, shooting at the riflemen above him. Miraculously he was unhurt. He was within a dozen feet of the top of the rise when the inevitable happened. Three rifles were turned upon him, and their lead slugs struck him. Joe was whirled around and hurled to the ground like a sack of meal. He dropped his gun, groped for it, found it again somehow, fought his way to his knees, steadied himself and leveled the weapon. The death-dealing rifles above him thundered again in unison. Joe was fairly riddled. His smashed, broken body rolled down the incline, collided with a jutting rock and came to a final stop.

Some hours later, Tex Murray, considerably more thoughtful than usual, sauntered out of the "K. C." for a breath of air. He halted in the open doorway and leaned against the doorframe. There were a dozen men idling near the hitching rail, and Tex listened to their conversation for a moment or two. He turned slowly, stopped and looked back over his shoulder when a horse clattered into town. The men at the rail looked up; their conversation ceased abruptly. The horse halted of his own accord, raised his head and whinnied. The body of a man toppled out of the saddle and crashed heavily to the ground.

Tex bounded into the street, collided with another man and sent him spinning away. He was the first to reach the crumpled body, the first to bend over the dead man. Presently the others crowded around him.

Gently, Tex Murray lifted his brother's body in his strong arms. When he came erect again, the other men stepped back without a word. He turned slowly, crushing

Tommy's bloodied head to his breast, held him tight, then trudged down the street, carrying his lifeless burden into his office.

12. An Eye for an Eye ★

THERE was a dim light in the kitchen. Canavan, striding from the barn to the back door, noticed it and shook his head. He opened the door noiselessly and peered in. The light in the lamp on the kitchen table had been turned down until it cast a narrow circle of yellowish light around the center of the table, leaving the rest of the room in darkness. In the old rocker beside the table was Beth Richards, and her bowed head told him that she was asleep. He closed the door, frowned when it voiced a tiny squeak, took off his hat and dropped it into a straight-backed chair that stood near the door.

"Beth," he said quietly.

The girl stirred. He came closer and bent over her.

"Beth," he said.

She moved again. He dropped to his knee beside her.

"Beth," he said for the third time.

She raised her head and opened her eyes. He laughed softly.

"Kinda past your turnin'-in time, ain't it?" he demanded, frowning at her.

"Oh, Johnny!" she said with relief in her voice. "I'm so glad you're back!"

He grinned at her boyishly.

"Why, Miss Richards! S'ppose someb'dy else was t' hear that! They might get ideas, y'know, an' that'd never do, would it?"

She flushed and got to her feet quickly to screen her embarrassment.

"You—you'll have some coffee, won't you?" she asked, averting her eyes. "I've kept a light under it for hours, so it should be good and hot."

"Oh, sure—an' thanks."

She started away but he straightened up quickly, caught her by the hand and slowly turned her around.

"Beth."

"Y—yes?"

He frowned again.

91

"Don't you know it's imp'lite not t' look at someb'dy when they're talkin' to you?"

Her head came up.

"Beth," he said and waited. Her eyes met his finally. "That's better. Beth, I've been doin' a lotta thinkin' 'bout you t'day. Think I'm gonna marry you."

"Oh—are you?"

He nodded vigorously, with complete finality.

"Uh-huh."

"Don't you think you ought to ask me first?"

"Oh, I dunno."

"Do you always do what you want and get what you want?"

"Wa—al, no, not always," he admitted. "But I c'n take a heap o' punishment b'fore I'm willin' t' admit that I've changed m' mind 'bout wantin' a thing."

"A thing! I'm sure I'm flattered!"

He grinned at her again.

"It's never been a girl that I've wanted b'fore," he explained, "so it's always been a thing. I'm sorry."

She had turned her head again.

"I'm gonna kiss you, Beth."

She did not answer.

"'Less you don't want me to," he concluded.

Her head jerked upward.

"Indeed!" she said icily. "Indeed!"

He caught her in his arms, held her close, crushed her lips with his, hungrily. She clung to him. Curiously neither one noticed it, but her arms were around him and they tightened there. He raised his head finally, looked down into her eyes and grinned at her.

"Johnny!" she whispered. He bent his head again and gently kissed her lips and her eyes. He pillowed her head on his chest and buried his face in her hair. "Johnny!"

"I know no one will believe me," a voice said from the doorway that led to the hall and stairway. They stepped apart quickly, awkwardly. Canavan, frowning, turned his head. Henry Comerford, attired in a nightshirt tucked into his pants, stood in the doorway. There was a wide grin on his face. "The fragrance of that coffee reached all the way upstairs, and when I couldn't resist it any longer, why, I simply had to come down and get some. I know you don't mind. And, incidentally, I hope I didn't interrupt anything."

There was no answer. Comerford shrugged his shoulders, sauntered over to the table and seated himself.

"Y'know," he mused, sitting back in the chair, "I haven't attended a wedding in more than ten years. I'm really going to look forward to this one."

There was a strange sound from Beth; it sounded like a choking gurgle. She wheeled suddenly and fled, flew up the stairs to her room.

Canavan emerged from the house early the next morning as Stanton rode up.

"H'llo," Canavan called, and the rancher reined in, wheeled and loped over to meet him. "How'd you fellers make out?"

Stanton swung himself out of the saddle.

"Oh, awright," he answered. He turned and watched for a moment as his horse jogged away toward the barn. "Leastways, we took care o' our jobs, both Carroll an' me. On'y neither uv us took any pris'ners."

Canavan eyed him questioningly.

"How come? Y'mean they got away at both places?"

Stanton shook his head.

"Nope," he replied. "S'ppose we kinda amble over t' th' c'rral where we c'n talk. Awright with you?"

"Yeah, sure."

They trudged away from the house, circled the barn and halted finally at the corral gates. Canavan leaned against the bars. Stanton was grim-faced now.

"We followed th' plan we'd worked out right down t' th' letter," he began again. "We s'rrounded th' place an' closed in. First thing I found was one o' them posters o' yourn nailed to a tree. It struck me kinda funny findin' it there. Anyway, it was full o' bullet holes."

"Go on."

Stanton moistened his lips.

"While th' others headed f'r th' house," he continued, "I swung over toward th' bunkhouse. I had th' extra guns, y'know, so's I could arm th' Parker boys when I busted in on 'em. Th' bunkhouse was empty."

Canavan looked surprised, but he made no comment.

"There's a kinda gully way down past th' barn," Stanton went on. "Notice it th' time you went t' see Parker? No? Wa—al, it ain't important right now, 'cept f'r one thing."

Canavan's hand gripped the rancher's wrist.

"Wait a minute," he said. "You ain't gonna tell me that—"

Stanton nodded grimly.

"That's right, Canavan," he said. "Parker's four men were layin' in th' gully. Th' way I figger it, they just fell into it. Anyway, they were dead. They'd all been plugged through th' back o' th' head."

"Why, th' dirty, murderin' hellions! So that's why you didn't take any prisoners, eh?"

"Uh-huh. I tol' th' boys what I'd found, an' they just about went wild. They blasted th' house t' bits, set fire to it an' drove Quarles's skunks out into th' open. Some o' th'm tried t' surrender. You shoulda heard 'em, Canavan, hollerin t' us t' give 'em a break. We gave 'em a break awright, leastways we gave decent folks a break. We killed every last one o' th' rats, nine in all."

"What about Carroll? What'd he find when he got t' Davis's place?" Canavan asked.

"Wa—al, seems like one o' Will's boys, feller named Garms, escaped an' hid out. Couple o' th' other boys, Sproul an' a kid named McVea, took t' smugglin' food to 'im. Quarles's men followed th'm one day. Th' boys, seein' that they were bein' trailed, doubled back an' run smack into another bunch o' Quarles's skunks. They tried t' make th' boys squeal, an' when they wouldn't give Garms away, they were hung up by their thumbs. When that didn't make 'em talk, they got a good wallopin'. Then they got th' water treatment. You know what that is, don'tcha?"

"Yeah, sure. Lettin' water drip down on their heads f'r hours at a time. I've heard tell o' some cases where th' victims fin'lly went plumb locoed. Th' Spanish used t' work that one down in Mexico."

"Quarles's treatment is worse. Water was squirted up their noses that left 'em chokin' an' more dead'n alive, then pailfuls were poured down their throat."

"I'll be damned!"

"But there ain't no point in goin' into that. Every one o' Will's boys got a sample o' some kind o' Quarles's treatment. When Carroll slipped into th' bunkhouse—an' it was a doggoned good thing f'r him th' guards were hittin' the bottle an' too busy t' notice what was goin' on—an' give th' boys th' guns he'd lugged along, they grabbed 'em an' went right t' work. What they did t' them so-an'-sos was nob'dy's business. Th' point is, they wiped 'em out. That's why Carroll come away empty-handed, too."

"Both o' you did a good job. Now here's what's been goin' on aroun' these parts. Charlie Baldwin's loaned me ten men, th' Gillens sent fifteen, an' between them an' what th' smaller outfits could spare, we've got some forty-five men all told."

"How 'bout Matt Fox an' Ed Hockett?"

Canavan shook his head.

"Neither one o' th'm even bothered t' answer th' note I sent th'm. Didn't s'prise me none, though. After th' tellin' off I gave Fox that day in Logan, I didn't expect him t' do anything, an' he didn't fool me. As f'r Hockett, I just don't know how t' figger him. There's somethin' about Hockett that kinda makes me wonder."

"What d'you mean?"

"It ain't somethin' I c'n put m' finger on. S'ppose we just call it a hunch an' let it go at that till I've got somethin' we c'n really talk about."

"Whatever you say, Canavan. This is your party an' I'm satisfied with th' way you're runnin' it. Say, where are those new men you were talkin' about? Whatcha plannin' t' do with 'em?"

Canavan grinned fleetingly.

"We're past th' plannin' stage. We're on th' job. I got th'm spread out aroun' Logan with orders t' shoot t' kill. Nob'dy's t' get into Logan or out uv it."

Stanton nodded approvingly.

"I get th' idea. You're gonna make Quarles hole up in Logan, then you're gonna whittle 'im down. Right?"

Canavan merely smiled his reply.

Dan Quarles started up the street from Tex Murray's office, when he heard a furious pounding of approaching hoofs. He looked up quickly and halted mechanically. Five horsemen came spurring into town at full gallop. Quarles's eyes widened when he saw eight riderless horses race in behind them. Murray, attracted by the clatter, emerged, too. He came striding up the street and stopped at Quarles's side.

"Five outa thirteen," he heard Quarles mutter.

"They musta run into somethin' too big f'r them t' handle," Murray said.

One of the horsemen spied Quarles, guided his mount away from the others, lashed him and sent him racing down the street. Pulling up in front of the two men in a dust-raising, skidding stop, he swung himself out of the saddle. Quarles, tight-lipped and grim-faced, eyed him.

"What happened?" he demanded curtly.

"Boss," the man answered breathlessly, "we run into

trouble an' we're danged lucky, th' five uv us that're left, that we managed t' get away with a hull skin."

Quarles frowned with impatience.

"What happened?" he repeated.

"Wa—al," the man began again, "we got outa Logan an' headed east, like you tol' us to. Reckon we musta covered mebbe six or eight miles, an' we were ridin' up a rise. We come to 'bout th' middle uv it, when all uva sudden all hell opened up on us. We didn't have a chance. They just about blasted us t' hell an' gone, an' those uv us that were left had t' turn tail an' get outa there while th' gettin' was still good."

"Anything else?" Quarles demanded coldly.

"Fr'm th' way we were gettin' lead poured into us," the man continued, "I got 'n idea th' ranchers've got Logan s'rrounded."

"You're loco!" Quarles snapped.

The man shrugged his shoulders.

"Could be, Boss," he said. "On'y I was out there ketchin' it, y'know, an' you weren't."

He turned on his heel, gripped the reins and pulled himself up into the saddle, wheeled and loped up the street.

"Mebbe he ain't loco," Murray said.

" 'Course he ain't," Quarles snapped. "I had t' tell 'im that so's he won't go spreadin' that story 'mong th' other men. Come on, let's go get us some coffee."

"Where?"

"Mother Jones's place'll do."

"She's closed 'er place up. There's a sign on 'er door an' it's got just one word on it—'Closed.' "

"H'm!"

"An' that joint up th' street," Murray continued, "that's closed, too."

Quarles said nothing as his narrowed eyes ranged the street.

"Y'know, Dan," Murray began again, "th' town ain't th' same no more. It's shot t' hell. Th' gen'ral store's gone an' now there ain't even a place t' eat. I don't like it. It's got me kinda worried. I got 'n idea we're gettin' awful close t' showdown time."

"We ain't beat by a long shot," Quarles said gruffly.

"Wa—al, who says we are?" Murray retorted. "I'm on'y tryin' t' tell you that we oughta get movin' again."

"Where are them forty men you said you had comin' in?" Quarles demanded.

96

"Oh, they'll be along, awright."

"Why ain't they here a'ready?"

"Takes time t' travel, don't it?"

"How long did it take you t' get here fr'm where they're at?"

"Oh, I dunno—"

"You made it in a day!"

Murray flushed and looked away. He turned again almost immediately.

"Hey, Dan—"

"Yeah?"

"You don't s'ppose, Dan, that—?"

"That somethin's happened to th'm?" Quarles asked. He shrugged his shoulders. "Could be."

"Yeah," Murray said thoughtfully. Now he looked disturbed. "I s'ppose it could be, awright."

Canavan, Stanton and Carroll huddled behind a huge white-faced boulder.

"Hear th'm now?" Canavan asked, turning.

Carroll nodded and tightened his grip on his rifle. Stanton inched his way forward, whipped off his hat and peered out quickly; then he withdrew his head.

"See 'em?" Canavan asked.

"Yep," Stanton said. "Eight or mebbe ten o' th'm."

"Where d'you s'ppose they're headed f'r?" Carroll asked.

"An' what'n blazes are they doin' all th' way up here?" Stanton added.

Canavan grinned.

"Don't ask me," he replied. "I'm on'y a stranger 'round these parts."

"What d'we do?" Carroll asked.

"There're on'y three uv us," Stanton said, "an' eight o' them, mebbe more."

"Th' odds don't mean anything in this case," Canavan said quietly. "You fellers'll have it all your own way shootin' down into th'm."

"Huh?" Stanton and Carroll said together.

"You're gonna hold th' fort," Canavan continued calmly, "while I work m' way around th'm. I'm gonna get me just one o' th'm, a live one."

The ranchers looked at each other, then at Canavan.

"What's th' idea?" Carroll asked.

"Yeah," Stanton said, "I don't savvy it."

Now the echoing clatter of racing hoofs on the range below them began to swell. Canavan hitched up his belt.

"Ain't got th' time t' go into it now," he said quickly. "I gotta get goin'. Give 'em a chance t' get real close, then pour it into 'em. They won't hang aroun' f'r long."

He stepped past them and dashed away.

A few minutes later, rope in hand, Canavan skidded to a panting stop behind a clump of brush and knelt down behind it. He raised his head once and looked up. Stanton and Carroll were atop a rise some three hundred feet southward. He could see no sign of them and he nodded approvingly.

"No sense in tippin' our hand," he muttered. "Time enough t' let 'em know we're aroun' when they get a dose o' hot lead poured into 'em."

He twisted around and peered down. A band of horsemen—there were eleven of them, strung out in single file—were riding swiftly past him. In another few minutes they would be mounting the incline. He sank down on his haunches and watched them patiently. They swung wide around an outcropping of wild juniper. Now they were in a more compact group, four abreast in the front line, five in the second, with the last two men bringing up the rear. Canavan nodded grimly.

"In just another minute," he muttered to himself.

He got up, tightened his grip on the rope, whirled away and scampered downward, swerving around rocks and small boulders. He skidded and slipped to his knees once or twice, but he scrambled to his feet each time without delay and plunged ahead. There was a sudden roar of rifle fire. He pulled up when he came to a small clump of brush, and dropped down behind it; after a moment he peered out. The onrushing horsemen had stopped. They were firing upward, and now Canavan saw two men topple out of their saddles, saw a horse rear up on his hind legs, saw his rider slip off his back, saw the horse crash over backwards.

Dust obscured his vision for a moment. It cleared presently, and he spotted the animal's rider again. The man had managed somehow to get out of the way of his tumbling horse. Another man fell out of his saddle. The first man stepped over him, reached for the loose-flying reins, grabbed for the saddle horn and pulled himself up astride the horse. As he wheeled the animal, a rifle cracked above him and the horse screamed, backed and fell suddenly, catapulting his rider through space. The man fell heavily, clumsily; he rolled away and dragged himself to his feet. He snapped a shot upward at the hidden riflemen; he drew a shot in reply and dropped his gun, turned away slowly, sank to his knees and simply pitched forward on his face.

The others in the group—Canavan ran his eye over them and counted seven—wheeled now, colliding with one another, swerved their mounts and started down the incline. Two or three of them turned in their saddles and fired at the concealed riflemen. A man fell forward in his saddle; a companion bumped him, and the wounded man slid off his horse's back, struck the ground and collapsed in a broken heap. The others spurred their horses and rode swiftly down the incline. One lone horseman, who seemed almost reluctant to leave the scene of the disastrous ambush, halted his mount, jerked his rifle out of his saddle sheath, raised it and fired twice. He lowered his rifle and, shaking his fist angrily, shouted something at Stanton and Carroll. He turned his head and watched his companions race away. He sheathed his rifle presently and rode slowly down the incline; now Stanton and Carroll held their fire. He clattered toward the brush behind which Canavan was waiting; in another minute he was abreast of it, then past it.

Canavan got to his feet. His right arm went back; it jerked suddenly and the rope shot away from him, swiftly, unerringly, like a striking snake. The noose opened and spun over the unsuspecting man's head; then it dropped, whirled around his body and tightened like a vise. The man was dragged out of his saddle. He struck the ground, rolled over, struggled to his feet and fought frantically to free himself from the rope.

"Hold it!" Canavan said curtly.

The man's struggles ceased. He was motionless for a moment, then turned his head slowly. Canavan's Colt gaped at him hungrily. Canavan stepped up to him, jerked the man's gun out of his holster, tossed it away and kicked at the payed-out rope.

"Pick it up!" he commanded.

The man scowled, bent stiffly and caught up the rope as Canavan, close to him, prodded him with his gun.

"Turn aroun' an' keep goin'," he said, nodding toward the incline.

Slowly they started up the grassy slope. They were halfway up when Stanton and Carroll, their rifles raised, arose and looked down. They stared hard and shifted their eyes from the man with the rope to Canavan, plodding upward behind him. Stanton laughed and said something to Carroll. Then both men lowered their rifles and sat down on the very edge of the rise.

13. Canavan Strikes Pay Dirt ★

THE early evening had been a cool one, with a promise in the not-too-distant offing of even brisker breezes as the night came on. Now it was night, and the promise was fulfilled. It was a cold night. It was a clear one, too, and the sky was filled with bright stars and a brilliant moon enriched a thousandfold by the backdrop of beautiful blue. The ground was hard and the pounding hoofs of the fleeting horse echoed like the steady beat of a muffled drum. Canavan was chilled and so was his horse. He turned up his jacket collar and settled himself deep in the saddle. There was no need for him to urge his horse on; the brisk air made the animal want to run, and run he did. They had covered many miles since sundown, but not once had they swerved from the northerly route they had set out to follow. A dust-swirling wind swept over them, and the horse whinnied protestingly; in a twinkling it was gone. Presently, too, the night air seemed even sharper than before, and Canavan, watchfully alert, took prompt note of it.

"Must be gettin' closer t' th' hill country," he told himself.

Another sudden wind burst upon them and, reaching up quickly, he pulled down his hatbrim over his smarting eyes. Then, as he looked up again shortly, tall, shadowy mountains loomed up ahead of him. As they whirled over the ground, the mountains seemed to grow larger, and finally their upper reaches appeared to be touching the blue sky. He checked his mount, tightening his grip on the reins to hold him down. He stopped altogether when he spied a huge, dark structure a hundred feet away. Canavan studied it interestedly.

"Uh-huh," he muttered, half aloud. "Reckon that's th' place awright."

He dismounted; it was an effort and it made him wince, for he was saddle-stiff. He stamped his feet on the ground, stretched himself, grimaced and hitched up his belt. He swerved away from the dark structure, halted again when he came upon a protective clump of bushes, tethered his horse there and started away on foot. He retraced his steps almost immediately, caught up a coiled rope that hung from the saddle horn, slung it over his shoulder, then trudged off again. He swung wide of the building, circling it warily before he closed in on it. He glanced skyward and frowned; he had hoped it would be a dark night. Unfortunately there had been no alternative; there was a job to do and no time to waste in the doing. He stopped and turned his eyes toward the front of the structure. It was a barn, the biggest barn he had ever seen. He was grateful now for the bright moon; he could see the wide doors, and despite the fact that he was still some distance off, he could see, too, that the doorway had been boarded up securely.

There was a boarded-up hayloft on the upper floor. A hoist bar that jutted straight out from a point above it caught and held his eye. He hitched up his pants again, drew a deep breath and started forward. But now he was even more watchful than before. He stopped and probed every sound and shadow. When he was satisfied that neither was man-made, he grunted inwardly and went on again. When a pebble crunched beneath his foot, he froze in his tracks, waiting to see whether anyone else had heard it. Each step brought him closer to the barn. He was some fifteen feet from the building when he stopped, seemed to gather himself together, then fairly flashed over the intervening space and flattened out against the shadowy wall. He waited, but nothing happened; there was no sound, and he relaxed a bit. Presently he stepped away from the wall, made his way around the building to the front of it, halted and looked up. He unslung his rope and backed off; then his arm shot out and the rope went hissing upward with a startlingly curious humming sound. It seemed to gather more and more speed as it hurtled higher, and for a brief moment it looked as though it would overshoot its mark. But suddenly what appeared to be a huge knot at the end of the lariat burst and became a noose, an ever-widening noose that spun above the hoist bar. The arc of its sweep grew larger. Canavan jerked his right arm and brought it downward to his side in a swift, decisive movement. Instantly the noose snapped shut, clamping itself around the bar.

He released the rope, allowing it to dangle loosely. He rubbed his hands together vigorously on his jacket and pants. Then he gripped the rope again and pulled it as hard as he could. It snapped taut and he pulled it again.

Then he seemed satisfied that the bar was secure. In another minute he was swinging upward, hand over hand. He swung against the building, twisting around in mid-air as he collided with it, hung there motionless for a moment, found a spot for his boot toes and dug in. He went on again presently, climbing and pulling himself upward. He stopped two or three times, dangling above the ground with the rope wound around one leg; when he felt refreshed, he simply kicked the rope away and pulled himself higher. In an incredibly short time he reached the hoist bar, swung a leg around it, gripped the bar with both hands, pulled himself up on it and perched himself there, breathless and tired.

He touched the boarded-up window with his boot toe; it refused to yield and he turned away from it. He managed somehow to get up on his feet. The edge of the sloping roof was fairly close and he inched his way along the bar until he reached it, clutched it, gripped it tightly and, with a super-human effort, pulled himself up on the roof. He lay there for a short time, fighting for breath; then he forced himself up. Slowly, carefully, he climbed, higher and still higher, and finally reached the top of the roof and straddled it as if it were a horse. A brief rest was all he permitted himself. There was still much to do, he told himself doggedly, and less time to do it in.

Slowly he moved along the roof. There was no particular purpose to this, he realized; it was simply due to his persistent urge to keep moving. He had hoped to be able to effect an entrance into the building; now he was aware of the futility of his stealthy effort. On and on he went, and finally he came to the far end of the roof and peered down. He found himself staring wide-eyed; there was no sheer drop from the roof to the ground below; actually he couldn't see the ground. What he could see was brush, and shale that glistened in the bright moonlight, and he gasped when he realized that the ground or something that would serve equally well was right below the level of the roof. He had but to reach out to touch it. The barn had been built into the side of a hill; if he had completed his circling of the structure, there would have been no need to climb it. He could have achieved the same result by simply trudging up the hillside.

He swung his legs over the edge of the roof, reached with his toes until he got a footing, slid off the roof, grabbed for the brush, clutched it and pulled himself away from the building. Slowly he tramped up the hill. There were half-buried rocks in his path and he tripped over them and stumbled to his knees, bruising them; each time, when he climbed to his feet, he cursed, first himself for his clumsiness, then Quarles. There were boulders of varying sizes and tree stumps just ahead, and tall trees beyond them. He made his way up to the trees, peered past them and stared hard. From then on, his movements covered inches; his forward or upward progress, moreover, was limited by caution. He dropped down on his hands and knees; he was at the edge of a deep canyon, and below it, hidden away in the very bottom of the encircling hills, screened by nature from probing eyes, was a circular valley.

"I'll be doggoned!" he muttered.

There was a campfire below him, too, and there were half a dozen men idling around it. Beyond them, on every side, were cattle. Suddenly the full impact of his discovery struck him.

"So that's what became o' th' rustled cattle!" he said, half aloud. Then an annoying question came into his mind. "But how'n hell did they got down there? Fr'm what I c'n see o' this danged layout, there's hills on every side an' nuthin' but a drop into that valley. Reckon they musta just flew 'em down there. That's th' on'y way I c'n figger it out."

He knelt there a little while longer, eyeing the men and the cattle. Finally he climbed to his feet, turned disgustedly and started down the hillside. He was scowling when he reached level ground again. He stalked around the building to the front, strode up to the boarded-up doorway, halted in front of it and glared at it. He stepped up to it, pushed it and muttered a curse when it refused to yield in the slightest. Something on the ground—a button—caught his eye; it gleamed with a metallic brightness in the moonlight. He was tempted to kick it away; instead he bent down to pick it up. He spied a tiny gleam of yellow light just below the bottom of the doorway and promptly forgot about the button. Cautiously he inched up to the doorway; a light, he decided, meant there was someone inside the barn. He was motionless for a moment, listening intently. Since he could hear nothing, he slid his hand under the boarded-up section and pulled it up gently. The boarding creaked a bit and started upward; he stifled a gasp of surprise. When he had raised it a dozen inches off the ground, he squatted down on his knees and peered into the barn.

There was a hand lantern on the floor, but he could see no one. He drew a deep breath, crept into the barn and looked about him quickly, warily. It was even bigger than he had thought. He got to his feet, loosened his gun in his holster, tiptoed past the lantern, went ten, twenty, thirty feet beyond it and stopped again. He chuckled inwardly; another ten or fifteen feet away was a ramp that led downward and out of sight. In that instant he sensed that he had solved the mystery, and he was jubilant. He went forward toward the head of the runway; there were hoofprints on the ground, confirmation of his discovery. There was no need for him to go farther. He turned and started toward the door. He looked up, grunted and stopped in his tracks. The boarding had been raised even higher to admit a girl and a huge man. They stared at him, and he at them. The man laughed. Canavan recognized him at once. It was big Ed Hockett.

"Reckon I called th' turn that time," he said to the girl. "Eh, Sue?"

The girl's face seemed vaguely familiar. Canavan eyed her. Then he knew her. She was Matt Fox's daughter. Hockett chuckled aloud and Canavan's eyes shifted quickly.

"Soon's I saw th' door'd been opened," he said, "I knew nob'dy but you woulda left it like it was."

"Then you musta been expectin' me."

"Yeah, sure," Hockett said quickly. "Figgered you'd find out about this place sooner or later, on'y I was hopin' it'd be a heck uva time later."

"Quite a setup you've got here, Hockett," Canavan said with affected casualness.

"Yep. Leastways it was awright till now. How'd you find it?"

"Oh, s'ppose we say it was just luck an' let it go at that."

The burly rancher shook his head.

"Let's not," he replied. "Let's say someb'dy told you 'bout it. That'd be a heap nearer th' truth, wouldn't it?"

"If that's th' way you want it," Canavan said with a shrug. "Now, if you folks don't mind, I'll kinda go on my way. It's a mite past my bedtime, y'know."

Hockett laughed again.

"Y'mean you wanna leave us so soon?" he chuckled. "Pull th' door down, Sue."

The girl moved alertly. She turned and pulled the door

without too much effort. It slid down and closed gently, shutting out the night.

"Don't try t' bite off more'n you c'n chew, Hockett," Canavan said quietly.

"I'm a big man," the rancher said with a grin. "You'd sure be s'prised at th' appetite I got. Sue, go close th' runway door fr'm th' outside. Mister Canavan an' me've got things t' talk about."

The girl stepped past him, stopping when Canavan moved.

"Might be better if she stayed," he said.

The girl turned slowly. Canavan, watching her out of the corner of one eye, saw her whirl. She snatched the lamp off the floor. Hockett fired from the hip, as did Canavan, and the two shots seemed to blend into a single shot. The lamp crashed against the wall, and the place was plunged into darkness. A shadowy figure flitted by and Canavan side-stepped nimbly, firing again in the direction of the doorway. Yellow flame spurted from Hockett's gun, and Canavan, watching for it, fired at it. There was a bellow from Hockett, proof that Canavan's bullet had struck him. Canavan moved again, swiftly and purposefully, refusing to furnish even an indistinct target, and snapped a lightning shot as he whirled around the place. Hockett's firing was now an indication of his rage; he blasted away and Canavan's Colt thundered a third time.

Now, too, another gun added its voice to the din, and Canavan sensed that it was Sue Fox's. He did not reply to it; he slipped away instead. But the girl quickly proved that she was nimble of brain as well as of foot, and she promptly adopted Canavan's methods for her own. She, too, moved, trying to keep pace with him. She fired a second time; there was a pause. Then she fired again but Canavan, watching, realized that she had moved with each shot. It was evident that she would prove a wily foe and that she was trying to force Canavan into a trap. Hockett, a slow mover and an equally slow thinker, finally became aware of what the girl was trying to do.

"Get behind 'im, Sue!" he yelled. "Get behind 'im!"

When he fired again, the flash from his gun indicated that he had shifted away from the door and that he was advancing slowly, hoping to trap Canavan between the girl and himself. Still there was no answering shot from Canavan. He seemed to have disappeared in the black darkness, but actually had reached a far wall. Flattened out against it, he quickly reloaded his gun. He turned his head slightly, toward the head of the ramp. He was not overworried about Hockett and the girl. He was confident that he could handle them and give them far more trouble than they could give him. His chief danger, he realized, lay in the men he had seen idling around the campfire. He wondered how long it would take them to reach the runway and come pounding up its length. Hockett, evidently thinking he detected some sort of movement, fired again. This time, however, Sue Fox held her fire, proof that she sensed trouble in the fact that Canavan refused to shoot back.

"If there was on'y some way o' gettin' outa here," Canavan muttered to himself, " 'side fr'm th' door an' th' runway!"

He holstered his gun, thrust his hands upward and was delighted when his fingers found a thick ceiling beam. He leaped upward, got a good grip on the beam and pulled himself up on it. There was some wooden planking just a foot or two beyond it and he swung onto it, realizing in that wonderful moment that he had reached the upper floor.

"Gotta take it easy," he whispered. "Gotta get outa here without lettin' 'em know it."

He crept along the planking. His caution paid dividends in short order; he found a gap in the flooring and circled it warily and safely. Hockett was completely impatient now; his gun thundered again, and this time Sue, spreading her fire to cover as much ground space as possible, fired four times. Canavan finally reached the upper-floor window that had also been boarded up. This time he did not attempt to force it; he pried it up instead, raised it about a foot and slid out on the sill. Reaching for his rope, which he had left dangling there, he gripped it and swung out. Swiftly he went down its length to the ground.

He was thirty feet from the barn when the front-door boarding was thrown up. He looked backward over his shoulder and saw big Ed Hockett burst out.

"Come on!" he heard the rancher yell. "He can't be far away yet. We oughta be able t' c'rral 'im!"

Canavan raced away, pounded up to the thicket where he had left his horse, vaulted into the saddle, wheeled and dashed off into the night.

14. The Handwriting on the Wall ★

MATT FOX was angry. His tight lips and his blazing eyes furnished a true reflection of his feelings. He paced his kitchen floor for a few minutes, wheeled suddenly and glowered at Hockett.

"You sure made one helluva fine mess o' things," he said gruffly, "but no more uva mess'n I shoulda expected uv you!"

"Aw, Matt—"

"Shut up!" Fox roared. "You get Canavan nailed down so's it's on'y a matter o' closin' in on 'im an' finishin' 'im off, an' you let 'im get away with a hull skin. You c'n bet on it, he'll be back by mornin' with a bunch o' men, an' that'll be th' beginnin' o' th' end."

Hockett did not answer.

"What gets me," Fox continued, "is that you saw his rope hangin' fr'm th' hoist. But did you do anything about it? Nope! Not a damned thing! You just let it hang there so's he could use it again t' make 'is getaway!"

"But doggone it, Matt," big Ed sputtered, "how was I t' know that, huh? I figgered that between me an' th' boys we'd get Canavan right smack in th' middle uv us an' blast 'im t' hell an' gone, an' that'd be that."

"You figgered!" Fox yelled. "You figgered with what, huh? You ain't got th' brains uva louse, an' you figgered!"

He turned away and paced the floor again.

"There oughta be somethin' we c'n do," Hockett said hopefully, yet not too certain.

Matt stopped and looked at Sue, who was standing at the window. His eyes brightened suddenly.

"Yeah," he said, "there is."

Hockett came quickly to his feet.

"Thought you'd hit on somethin'," he said quickly. "You allus seem able t' come up with some idea."

Fox turned and looked at him.

"We've got on'y one chance o' stoppin' Mister Canavan in 'is tracks."

"Huh? What d'you mean, Matt?"

"We gotta hit 'im through someb'dy else."

"I don't savvy it yet."

"What's so s'prisin' about that?" Fox retorted scornfully. "Look, you dumb, overstuffed buff'lo, who means more t' Canavan th'n anybody else, huh?"

"Comerford?" Hockett asked.

"No, damn it!"

"Dad means Beth Richards," Sue said, turning away from the window.

" 'Course I do!" Fox said heatedly. "Y'know, Hockett, I dunno why'n hell I didn't make you tie up with Canavan's bunch. We'da had a chance then."

"What's your plan, Dad?" Sue asked.

"Wa—al, if we c'n get our hands on Beth, we c'n use her when we hafta make a deal with Canavan. Get it?"

"Yes, certainly."

"How d'you know there's somethin' b'tween Beth an' Canavan?" Hockett asked.

"I thought everyone knew that," Sue said coldly. "He's been her shadow ever since he came here."

"Y'mean," Fox said cuttingly, "that everybody knew that 'cept Hockett. He don't even know enough t' come in outa th' rain."

"How do you plan to get to Beth?" Sue asked.

"Through you," her father answered calmly. "You an' her 've been friends f'r a long time. We'll send someb'dy down t' her place with word that you're sick an' that you want her t' come up here an' kinda lend a hand. That'll do it."

"Oh!"

"Get th' idea now, Mister Hockett?" Fox asked, glancing in Ed's direction.

"Yeah, sure," Hockett said quickly, enthusiastically. "An' it's awright, too."

"If Canavan doesn't get to her before we do," Sue remarked, "and spoil our little plan."

"That's one o' th' chances we've gotta take," her father retorted.

He turned on his heel and trudged out.

Dan Quarles sat at the small desk in the private office at the rear of the "K. C." There was a huge placard spread out before him and he scowled at it as he read it for the fifth time.

Quarles pushed the placard away. He got to his feet, opened the office door and sauntered into the café itself. There were three men at a corner table; the bar itself was deserted. The men looked up for a moment. They turned their heads again when Quarles halted at the bar and leaned over it.

> The following names have been stricken from the "wanted" list of criminals known to have been given refuge in the town of Logan:
>
> | | |
> |---|---|
> | Monk Smiley | Pete Waters |
> | Johnny Galvin | Len Burt |
> | Tex Rich | Dan McHugh |
> | Gale Brewer | Steve Higgins |
> | Gunner Sundstrom | Gay Lord |
> | Hap Fletcher | Leo Sands |
> | Joe Hicks | Ford Harmon |
> | Jess McDowell | Hy Hill |
> | Paddy McDowell | Pat Sloan |
>
> Four men, slain while resisting attempts of law enforcement officers to apprehend them, have not yet been identified.
>
> It may also be reported that two groups of men headed in the general direction of Logan were intercepted by law enforcement officers operating west of Logan. The first group was routed, and left eleven dead, four prisoners, two of whom died of their wounds; the second group, numbering twenty-one men, was surrounded and captured intact. Their names will be made public at a later date.
>
> Of general interest is the fact that six ranches overrun by Quarles's units have been recaptured and the lawless intruders, to the last man, wiped out.
>
> CITIZENS' COMMITTEE
FOR LOGAN

"Pete!" he called.

The bartender did not answer.

"Pete!" Quarles called again.

"Mebbe he went down t' th' cellar, Boss," one of the men at the table said loudly.

Quarles turned and leaned back against the bar.

"Any o' you fellers know how that sign come t' be in my office?" he asked.

"Y'mean th' one with all them names on it?" a man asked. "Th' one with that Smiley feller's name on top?"

"Yeah, that's th' one."

"Wa—al," the man began, "this mornin', when I was standin' outside, four o' our horses come lopin' into town. All o' th'm had signs like th' one you got hangin' fr'm their saddles. I brung one o' th' signs in here an' Pete made me give it t' him. Reckon he must be th' one who put it in your office."

"What was that about four o' our horses?"

"Huh? Oh, th' horses. They were ours awright. One o' th'm was a big white mare. I'd know that critter anywheres. She used t' b'long t' Len Burt. Then there was Hap Fletcher's horse, th' one with that one eye, Pat Sloan's sorrel an' Johnny Galvin's black."

Quarles had nothing more to say. He turned away from the bar and started away toward his office. Then he stopped midway and looked back over his shoulder.

"Gettin' late," he said gruffly. "You fellers better call it a day an' turn in."

The three men pushed their chairs back from the table, climbed to their feet, hitched up their belts and turned toward the street door.

"Any o' you seen Tex Murray aroun' t'night?" Quarles asked.

One man, a tall fellow with a red face, nodded.

"He was in 'is office when I passed there 'long about ten o'clock," he said.

Quarles's eyebrows arched in surprise.

"He was?"

The man nodded again.

"Yep, an' it looked t' me like he was busier'n hell."

Quarles eyed him.

"What d'you mean?" he demanded.

"He was emptyin' out th' desk drawers, piling all th' stuff on top o' his desk."

"What'd he do with it then?"

"Saw 'im stuffin' some uv it into a gunny sack."

Quarles was silent for a moment. Then he looked up again.

"Awright. You fellers trot along. Tex'll prob'ly show up by an' by."

The three men went out. Quarles was motionless. He heard a footstep and turned quickly. It was Pete Collins, the bartender.

"Where you been?" Quarles demanded.

Collins looked surprised.

"Down th' cellar," he replied. "Why? Somethin' th' matter?"

"Nope. I was just wonderin'."

"Oh," Collins said, and his tone indicated his relief. "Y'know, Boss, we're b'ginnin' t' run short o' things."

"What kind o' things?"

"Most everything, fr'm beer t' bacon. Kinda tough on us with all th' stores shut down, y'know. Used t' be all we had t' do was ask Gorman or one o' th' others, even Mother Jones, an' f'r every one uva kind you asked f'r, they brung us two. Now they're gone an'—"

"I know," Quarles interrupted curtly. "I know."

"I was on'y tryin' t' tell you what was what, Boss."

"Awright. F'rget it. We'll be gettin' stuff in any day, now."

Collins nodded, turned and went behind the bar.

"You seen anything o' Murray t'night?" Quarles said.

"Yeah, sure," the bartender answered. "Ain't he back yet?"

"Ain't he what?"

"I said, ain't he back yet? I saw 'im ridin' off 'long about midnight."

"Oh, yeah? Which way'd he go?"

"On'y way he could go when he went past here—east."

"'Bout midnight, eh?"

Collins nodded.

"You wasn't around, Boss. He went into your office an' stayed in there f'r a few minutes. Now that I think uv it, I don't even r'member seein' 'im come out uv it. All I do r'member is lookin' up like I allus do these days when I hear a horse an' seein' 'im ride past."

"Was he carryin' anything?"

"Huh? Oh, yeah, seems t' me there was a big, fat gunny sack swingin' fr'm 'is saddle horn. Didn't seem important; that's why I didn't mention it right off."

Quarles nodded mutely, slowly.

"Boss," Collins began again.

"Yeah?" Quarles asked without looking up.

"Boss, I dunno what this is all about, but—"

"Yeah?" Quarles said and looked up.

"There's been a helluva lot o' whisperin' goin' on among th' men these last two days. Thought you oughta know 'bout it."

"Thanks," Quarles said and turned away. "Keep your ears open, Pete," he said over his shoulder, "an' lemme know if you hear anything."

111

"Sure, Boss."

Quarles went past his office to the storeroom at the rear, made his way through the darkened room, turned and went down the narrow flight of stairs to the basement. At the landing he caught up a hand lantern, fumbled with it for a moment and struck a match. Presently a light flamed in the lantern. He carried it away with him to the dark, far end of the cellar. He stopped in front of an iron door, produced a huge key, inserted it in the lock and turned it. Grasping the handle on the door, he pulled hard. The door squeaked open. Quarles pushed against it, opened it wide, raised the lantern and peered into the room. It was empty and he nodded to himself, lowered the lantern, backed a bit, pulled the door and swung it shut. He locked it and tramped away, halted when he came to the stairway, blew out the light and set the lantern on the floor. Presently his heavy step sounded on the stairs. A door opened and closed behind him.

There was a light in the Richards kitchen when Canavan rode around to the rear of the house.

"Waitin' up again f'r me," he muttered and smiled. "She sure is swell, doggone it!"

He dismounted, strode quickly to the door, opened it as noiselessly as he could, and poked his head inside. His eyes widened. Seated at the table was Tex Murray; standing behind him, gun in hand, was Carroll. There was a quick step from the connecting doorway, and Stanton, his gun half drawn from his holster, appeared.

"Oh!" he said and stopped. "Glad you got back. Didn't wanna keep our comp'ny waitin' up f'r you all night."

Canavan closed the door behind him.

"Mister Murray," Stanton said with a wink, "is here t' see if he c'n make a deal f'r 'imself. Interested or d'you want us t' take care o' him?"

Canavan grinned back at him and pushed his hat up from his eyes.

"What's th' proposition, Murray?" he asked. "An' does your side-kick Quarles know what you're up to?"

Tex turned slowly in his chair.

"Quarles don't know anything 'bout this," he said simply.

"I see," Canavan said. "An' th' proposition?"

Murray cleared his throat.

"First off," he began, "whether you b'lieve it or not, all th' killin's an' things goin' on aroun' Logan ain't any o' my doin's. Quarles is th' boss an' tells th' boys what t' do, so that leaves me in th' clear."

"Go on," Canavan commanded.

Stanton dragged a chair away from the table, swung it around and sat down.

"Next," Murray continued, "I ain't wanted by anybody f'r anything. I tied up with th' wrong feller, an' that's all."

"I'll say you did!" Stanton said and laughed.

"Go on, Murray," Canavan said. "It's late an' we wanna get us s'me sleep."

Murray cleared his throat again.

"I'm here t' offer you a fair proposition," he went on. "I'll turn over everything I got in writin' on Quarles. An' I got plenty, b'lieve me."

"An' what d'you want in r'turn?" Canavan asked.

"A free ticket t' where I'm headed f'r," Murray replied calmly, "California."

Canavan was silent.

"Actu'lly," Tex went on, "I don't hafta ask f'r anything. I ain't done anything an' nob'dy c'n say I have, either. But I'd rather have it this way so's everything'll be on th' up-an'-up. What d'you say?"

"No deal, Murray."

Stanton laughed, got to his feet and spun his chair away.

"There's your answer, mister," he said loudly. "You heard 'im. You're in this thing with Quarles right up t' your neck, an' when he swings, so do you."

"You fellers ride back with 'im," Canavan said, turning first to Stanton, then to Carroll. "See that he gets back t' Logan an' t' Mister Quarles."

"Sure," Stanton said. "Come on, Murray. We got places t' go."

Murray rose.

"Look," he said, "I'll do better'n I offered to. Dan gave me ten thousand dollars a couple o' weeks ago. You fellers split it among th' three o' you any way you like. Awright?"

Canavan shook his head.

"No," he said curtly. "Get 'im outa here."

Carroll prodded Murray with his gun. Tex shrugged his shoulders. Canavan jerked the door open. Stanton caught up his hat from a chair in the corner of the room, clapped it on his head and went out. Murray trudged out heavily, Carroll, his gun leveled, following at his heels. Stanton returned a moment later.

"F'rgot t' tell you," he said, "feller fr'm Matt Fox's outfit come after Beth an' she went off with 'im. Seems Sue is bedded down with somethin' or other an' wanted Beth t' take care o' her f'r a few days. Beth said t' tell you."

Canavan stared at him.

"S'matter?" Stanton asked.

Canavan hitched up his belt.

"Not a damned thing," he said gruffly. "That was just a trick f'r Fox t' get Beth in his hands. There ain't a damned thing th' matter with Sue. I know b'cause I saw 'er t'night."

"I'll be doggoned!"

Canavan brushed past him, raced to his horse, swung himself up into the saddle, wheeled and dashed away.

15. Honor Among Thieves ★

THE night had gone and its obscuring veil of darkness had been whisked away. The sky that had been filled with blue and silver was empty and drab, the timeless void between night and day. There was stirring in the air. For a breathless moment there was a curious, startling hum like tiny, fleeting voices; then a faint light like that of a distant, sputtering candle held aloft in the wind gleamed for an instant on the horizon. In another instant it was gone. A brisk wind whipped over the range, whirled the dust through the street and whined away southward, and everything was still again. Logan slept soundly—all save one man. Dan Quarles, a motionless figure in the open doorway of the "K. C.," was the man. Until Pete Collins had locked up and turned in, Quarles had kept to his office. He had looked up once to find the bartender watching him out of the corner of his eye; he had scowled and Pete, flushing awkwardly, had quickly turned away. Finally, when he could stand it no longer, he had ordered the man to lock up.

"Awright, Boss," Pete had answered, "if you want me to. On'y thing is, I ain't sleepy yet. B'sides, s'pposin' you want somethin', huh? Who's gonna get it f'r you then?"

"I won't be wantin' a thing. You go ahead an' turn in."

"Yeah, sure, Boss, in just one minute. Wanna get these danged glasses outa th' way an' up on th' shelves b'fore somethin' happens t' th'm. It's th' doggonedest thing how s' many o' th'm get busted inside uva day's time. On'y yesterday, I—"

"F'r th' luvva Mike, Pete!"

Collins had grinned sheepishly. But fifteen minutes later he was still behind the bar. Quarles, scowling with annoyance and impatience, came striding out of his office and Pete looked up.

"I'm about done, Boss," Pete said quickly. He turned and flipped a wet bar rag over the spigot of a beer barrel. He looked up. "C'n I fix you a drink b'fore I go upstairs? Somethin' extra special, huh?"

"No. If I want anything later on, I'll fix it m'self. G'wan, get outa here."

Pete shrugged his shoulders. He came around the bar, trudged to the door and turned the key.

"Turn out th' lights too."

Slowly, more slowly than he had ever moved before, Collins put out the lights. Then, reluctantly, he went upstairs.

Now there was a sudden brightening in the sky and it seemed as though a million candles had been touched off. A light spread over the horizon and deepened. It was morning. Quarles straightened up; he thought he had heard a hoofbeat. He was motionless, listening; then he nodded. He hadn't imagined it at all. Presently a horseman appeared, riding slowly into Logan. It was Tex Murray, and he looked over at the "K. C.," spied the man in the doorway, checked his horse and stopped him. Quarles did not move. For a brief minute the two men looked at each other, each seemingly waiting for the other to speak. But Quarles was the stronger; he held his tongue. Murray wheeled his horse, rode up to the "K. C." door and dismounted heavily.

"I'm back," he said.

Quarles smiled fleetingly.

"Figgered you would be," he said. "On'y I didn't know f'r sure whether you'd be dead or alive."

There was a slight pause now.

"I've been a damned fool, Dan," Tex said shortly.

Quarles's eyebrows arched.

"That so?"

Murray nodded slowly.

"A heap bigger fool th'n I ever thought I'd be," he continued. "I don't even know what come over me. It just— wa—al, it just happened, an' when I kinda snapped out uv it, I come back quick's I could."

There was no comment from Quarles.

"I dunno what it is," Tex went on dully. "Mebbe it's th' kid. I ain't been th' same since he was killed. Anyway, it wasn't me that done what I done t'night. It couldn't be, 'cause soon's I come to an' realized what was goin' on, I turned aroun' an' come hotfootin' it back. I wouldn't hitail it on you if I hadda swing f'r it. You know that."

Quarles was still silent.

"There's somethin' else, Dan."

"Yeah?"

Murray moistened his lips.

"I took some o' your dough, too," he said; "that bank dough, y'know."

"I know."

"It's in th' sack," Murray said, nodding toward his horse. Quarles's eyes followed Tex's nodding head. "I ain't touched it. Ain't even looked at it. Wanna put it back th' same way."

Quarles hooked his thumbs in his gun belt.

"Musta covered a lotta ground since midnight," he remarked. "See anybody on th' range?"

Murray shook his head.

"Nope. Nob'dy."

Quarles's eyebrows arched again.

"H'm," he mused. "An' I thought Canavan had us pretty well s'rrounded."

"I wanna put th' dough away," Murray said.

He turned, lifted the sack off his saddle horn, put it down on the ground, bent over it and untied it. When he straightened up again, his arms were filled with yellow canvas bags. Quarles eyed them, looked at Murray and grinned.

"You sure fixed y'self up awright," he said lightly and laughed.

Tex grinned sheepishly.

"Go ahead," Quarles said, and Murray stepped past him and into the café. "Wait a minute."

Murray stopped and turned around slowly.

"Dump 'em on th' bar," Quarles said. He stepped inside, too, and came around the bar. "Stack 'em up while I rustle up a drink f'r us."

Tex heaped the bags on the bar and turned away.

Quarles uncorked a bottle, placed it on the bar and followed it with two glasses. He filled his glass, put down the bottle and nodded toward it.

"Go ahead," he said.

Murray poured himself a drink. His hand was unsteady and he spilled some of the liquor on the bar. Quarles watched him, laughed again and raised his glass.

"Here's mud in your eye, Tex."

"An' here's t' you, Dan. You're a swell feller."

"Thanks."

They drained their glasses and put them down again.

"How 'bout another one?" Quarles asked.

Murray shook his head.

"Nope. One's just about all I c'n handle right now."

Quarles did not press his invitation. He simply shrugged his shoulders. Murray hitched up his belt.

"I'm gonna turn in, Dan. I'm plumb tuckered out."

"Yeah, reckon you've had a big night, Tex."

The sheriff turned toward the door. Quarles came around the bar and followed him outside.

"See you later," Tex said over his shoulder, mounted and jogged off.

Quarles, his thumbs hooked in his gun belt, followed him with narrowed eyes. He jerked out his gun; he looked down. The gunny sack lay at his feet. He kicked it; it was empty and he smiled grimly. He raised his gun and pulled the trigger. The shot echoed the length of the deserted street. Murray fell forward in his saddle. Quarles's gun roared a second time, and Tex sagged brokenly and toppled into the street. Quarles, laughing, fired a third time and Murray's body threshed about for a moment. Quarles emptied his gun, three final vicious shots that tore into the crumpled body of the man who had sought to betray him.

Blue smoke swirled around Quarles. He holstered his gun, turned and tramped back to the "K. C." He stopped at the bar; he was tired now and his every movement was slow and labored. He leaned over the bar, reached for the bottle he had left there, poured himself another drink and gulped it down; his eyes lit on Tex's glass and he frowned. He put down his own glass and picked up the other, which he studied for a moment and turned over in his hand. Suddenly he whirled, drew back his arm and hurled the glass into the street.

He started away toward the rear, halted and retraced his steps. He picked up one of the canvas bags, hefted it, untied it and tipped it over. Tightly packed rolls of poker chips and thick wads of cut paper, packaged together like wads of bank notes, spilled out over the bar.

He shook his head, grunted, turned away from the bar a second time and trudged wearily into the dim depths of the café.

The shadowy figure of a man emerged from a cluster of trees and moved swiftly toward the darkened bunkhouse. The man inched his way around the structure to the front. He stumbled in the darkness over a coil of rope, caught it up and looped a noose at one end. He carried the rope away with him, dropped below the level of the bunkhouse window and reached the door. He slipped the noose around the doorknob and jerked it tight, then backed away, paying out the rope and circling the building. Finally, he tied the rope in a secure knot.

"That oughta keep Fox's hired hands fr'm bustin' out," he muttered, "an' hornin' in on things."

The ranch house itself, a sizeable structure two stories high, loomed up some fifty or sixty feet away. Canavan eyed it, studying it for a minute. Like the bunkhouse, it was completely darkened.

"H'm," he muttered. "Gonna take a lot o' searchin' around t' find out where that ol' hellion's got Beth locked up."

He covered the intervening space to the house swiftly. When he reached it, he flattened out against a side wall. He started toward the rear but drew back instantly when he heard a heavy step. Then a man appeared and came down the path that ran alongside the house. Canavan caught his breath; he jerked out his gun and gripped it. The man came abreast of him, and Canavan shifted the gun; the man passed him, and Canavan stepped out behind him. His gun flashed upward and came whirling down. It thudded on the man's head. He grunted and toppled; Canavan caught him in his arms and lowered him to the ground.

In a brief minute the man was trussed up; his wrists were bound behind his back with his pants belt, and his handkerchief was jammed into his mouth to prevent an outcry when he regained consciousness. Canavan rolled him over on his face, pushed him into the shadows at the very foot of the side wall and then straightened up.

Swiftly he made his way to the rear. The back door,

he discovered, was ajar, and he decided that the man whom he had knocked out was a guard posted just inside the kitchen to prevent a sudden swooping-down planned to liberate Beth. He slipped into the house, moved forward cautiously, felt his way around the kitchen table and the drawn-up chairs, and finally emerged into a hallway. There was a bedroom opposite the kitchen and he probed it guardedly. The heavy breathing of a man who lay sprawled out on the bed reached him as he opened the door. He closed it again noiselessly. The stairway to the upper floor was farther front. Canavan reached it presently, mounted the first step and froze when a floor board squeaked beneath his weight.

After a minute he went on again, slowly and carefully. He was relieved when he finally reached the landing. He moved about the floor on tiptoe until he found a door. He turned the knob gently. The door opened the barest bit and he listened intently. He could hear deep, labored breathing, and he decided that it was Fox's room.

"Ol' coot!" he muttered to himself. "I oughta go in there an' wring his ornery neck."

He closed the door carefully, bruising his finger, and cursed inwardly. He moved away and collided with a chair. He picked it up, turned and laid it on its side directly in front of Fox's door, grinning fleetingly.

"It'd sure be a pity if he was t' come gallopin' outa his room," he mused, "an' trip over th' chair an' bust that fool neck o' his. That'd save me th' trouble o' doin' it for 'im."

He went on again. There was another door close by and he stopped here, listened at the keyhole for a moment, tried the knob, turned it and opened the door. He could hear nothing. Then there was a slight stirring in the darkness of the room, and he attributed it to someone's turning over in bed. This, he decided, was a girl's room, probably Sue's. It would be expecting too much of fate and chance to find that it was Beth's room instead. A board squeaked beneath him and he stiffened instantly. There was another stirring on the bed.

"Johnny!"

He was across the room in a single stride and knelt down beside the bed.

"Oh, Johnny!" Beth whispered.

She was in his arms. She clung to him.

"You awright, honey?"

"Yes, of course!"

119

"How'd you know it was me?"

There was no immediate reply. Beth couldn't answer. His lips had found hers and they were warm and eager.

"I knew you would come for me," she whispered presently. "That's why I knew it was you the moment I heard the door open."

There was another moment of silence. He kissed her again.

"Don't you think we ought to be getting out of here?" she whispered shortly.

"Huh? Oh, yeah, sure. You hop outa bed an' climb into your clothes. I'll kinda keep 'n eye on things outside. An' make it snappy, will yuh?"

A few minutes later Beth tiptoed out of the room. Canavan led her to the stairway.

"Hang on t' me," he whispered. "If anything happens, back away fr'm me so's I'll have room t' move aroun' in. But don't get too far away."

"I won't!"

He squeezed her hand. They started down the stairs. There was a sudden noise on the lower floor. A door was flung open. They halted abruptly.

"Matt!" a voice yelled. "That you?"

"Hockett," Beth whispered in Canavan's ear.

"Oh, yeah?"

"Matt!" Hockett's voice boomed again.

A door on the upper floor burst open. There was a loud crash as Fox fell over the chair.

"Come on!" Canavan hissed.

They fled down the stairs.

"Who's that?" Hockett yelled. "Talk up, y'hear, b'fore I start blastin'!"

"Shoot!" Fox screamed from the upper floor. "Shoot, yuh danged fool!"

A gun thundered deafeningly and a bullet plowed into the hallway wall just beyond the stairway. Another gun roared in answer. There was a gasp, a wheezing, then a dull thud.

Canavan and Beth groped their way past the stairway. He stopped when he stumbled over a sprawled body, guided Beth away from it and led her through the kitchen to the back door.

"Hockett?" she asked breathlessly.

"I musta got 'im with that one shot," he whispered in reply.

They slipped out of the house. Hand in hand they

120

raced around it to the front, swerved away from it and dashed toward the bunkhouse. There was a yell from within.

"Hey!" a voice cried. "Someb'dy let us outa here, will yuh?"

The bunkhouse window was suddenly thrown open. Canavan fired, shattering the windowpane, which fell in with a crash. They raced past the structure and plunged into the shadowy cluster of trees beyond. Canavan helped Beth to mount his horse, climbed up behind her, wheeled and dashed away southward.

16. The Reckoning

THE furious pounding of a horse's hoofs echoed in the morning air, and Canavan opened the kitchen door and peered out. Stanton came whirling up to the house, pulled his lathered horse to a stiff-legged stop and came sliding out of the saddle.

"Canavan!" he yelled, dashing up to him. "It's all over but th' shoutin'!"

Canavan grinned.

"Hurray!" he answered. "What's all over?"

"Quarles's men've pulled outa Logan," Stanton panted in explanation. "They've headed westward. What d'you think o' that?"

Canavan's eyebrows arched.

"So he's holdin' th' fort by 'imself," he mused.

"Wa—al, no," Stanton said. "Not exactly. Matt Fox an' that daughter of his are there with Quarles."

"When'd they show up?"

"Oh, a couple o' hours ago. You musta got Hockett awright, or else he'da been with 'em, too. Reckon we've come t' showdown time, eh?"

"Yep, this is it awright."

"It's our move now. What d'you want us t' do?"

Canavan's face was grim.

"Go back t' your men," he said with finality. "I don't want either Quarles or Fox t' get outa Logan."

"They won't!" Stanton said quickly. "They're there t' stay."

"What about Carroll?"

"He went northward like you tol' 'im to. Took twenty

121

men with 'im, an' th' chances are by now that danged hidden valley is wide open an' th' cattle out uv it."

"Swell. You better get goin'."

Stanton eyed him curiously.

"In a minute," he replied. "But what about Quarles an' Fox? We c'n move in on 'em th' minute you say th' word."

Canavan shook his head.

"I'm goin' into Logan."

Stanton's eyes widened.

"Y'mean—by y'self?"

"Uh-huh."

"What's th' big idea?"

"It's my job," Canavan said simply.

"Your job?" the rancher echoed. "What d'you mean, it's your job? I don't savvy that."

"You will, Stanton, you will."

"Yeah? When'll that be?"

Canavan grinned at him and patted him on the back.

"Oh, by an' by."

Stanton frowned.

"Look," he began again, "there's two o' th'm, Quarles an' Fox. Then there's Sue Fox, an' she's s'pposed t' be able t' handle a gun a heap better'n her ol' man c'n. What's more—an' you know it well's I do—she ain't afraid t' use 'er gun, either. So that makes th' odds three t' one."

"Sounds lots worse'n it actu'lly is."

"Mebbe," Stanton grunted. "But how 'bout me taggin' along with you, huh?"

Canavan shook his head again.

"Nope," he said. "You go back like I said b'fore. An' don't go worryin' about me."

"Awright," Stanton said heavily. "You're th' boss. An' if that's th' way you want it, that's th' way it's gonna be."

He turned on his heel, went back to his horse, mounted him and rode away. Canavan closed the door behind him, hitched up his pants and started off toward the barn.

"Johnny!"

He halted and looked back over his shoulder. Beth came flying toward him from the kitchen.

"Johnny," she said quickly, her anxious eyes probing his face, "you're not going after Quarles and Fox alone, are you?"

"H'm, eavesdroppin', eh?"

"Please!"

He smiled down at her.

"Sure I'm goin' after th'm. But don't you fret none. It ain't in th' cards f'r them t' do anything t' me, honey."

"But, Johnny, suppose they should?"

He bent swiftly and kissed her on the tip of her nose.

"They won't," he said simply. "What's more, I'll be back here b'fore you know it. Say—"

"Yes, Johnny?"

"Was that th' makin's uva blueberry pie I saw on th' kitchen table when I come past?"

She nodded; a smile flashed over her lips. In an instant it was gone.

"Gee, I c'n almost taste it now. Y'better see to it that I get th' biggest hunk, y'hear?"

"You—you'll be careful, won't you?"

"Look," he said quietly, "I love you. You know that. There ain't anything or anybody that's gonna stop me fr'm doin' what I've gotta do an' fr'm comin' back here."

He strode away. Beth turned slowly and went back to the house. Henry Comerford and Colonel Wynn emerged from the barn as Canavan approached it.

"Wasn't that Stanton who left here just a few minutes ago?" Comerford asked.

Canavan nodded.

"Any news?" Comerford asked. "I've a vacant spot in the obituary column for a certain person named Quarles, you know."

"I know, an' mebbe you'd better get somethin' whipped up f'r 'im."

Comerford's eyes widened.

"You mean that?" he asked.

"Quarles's men have pulled out on 'im," Canavan replied. "Accordin' t' th' way I figger it, that's th' beginnin' o' th' end."

"I'd certainly enjoy seeing Mister Quarles get his comeuppance," the newspaper editor said.

"You stick t' your knittin'," Canavan said. "You're a heap handier with them presses o' yourn than y'are with a gun, an' this is th' time f'r a gun t' do all th' talkin'."

He pushed past them into the barn and reappeared presently, leading his horse. Quickly he saddled his mount. He drew his gun, broke it, shoved it down into his holster, vaulted into the saddle, wheeled and rode away. Comerford and Colonel Wynn had watched him silently; now they plunged into the barn. Presently both men rode out astride their horses. Colonel Wynn had a heavy rifle slung over his shoulder. They rode around the barn, spurred their horses and dashed away eastward.

Canavan swung wide of Logan, approached it finally from the south and entered it from the west. He dismounted and left his horse in an alleyway far down the street. Logan was hushed and deserted. There were shattered windows in the stores along the street, and the town had taken on a ghostlike appearance. There was a horse in the street; a dozen feet beyond him lay an outstretched figure. Canavan eyed it wonderingly. He started up the street; every time he came to an alley, he stopped, peered into it and went on again. He crossed the street before he came to the sheriff's office, edged his way up to it, stole a quick look into it through the window, stepped up to the door and burst inside, his gun leveled and ready. But the office, too, was deserted, and he came out of it shortly. He glanced across the street; the curtains in Mother Jones's place were tightly drawn over the window.

He crossed the street again, glancing at the bank and at the *Bugle* office next door to it. There was no sign of life in the hotel; a window on the upper floor gaped without a pane of glass in its frame. He passed the vacant store in which he had voted, and the spot on which John Richards had died. It seemed so long ago. He stopped abruptly when he thought he had heard something, and quickly stepped into a near-by doorway. He peered out shortly and saw Sue Fox ride out of the alley that ran alongside the "K. C.," saw her wheel her horse and pull up directly in front of the café.

"H'm," Canavan said half aloud, eyeing her, "there's th' hellcat 'erself. She's sure a chip off'n th' old block. Wonder what she's up to now. I'd sure like t' give 'er a good whack on 'er fanny. Might do 'er some good."

The girl turned in her saddle.

"Well?" she called impatiently.

There was no response to her question. Canavan saw her tighten her grip on the bridle.

"All right, you fools!" she screamed furiously. "You can stay here and die for all I care! I'm going!"

She spurred her horse and he bounded forward. The horse that Canavan had seen in the street whinnied and started toward Sue. She swung her hand threateningly and the horse hastily shied away. In another minute she had swept out of town.

"G'bye an' good riddance," Canavan muttered. "Now

it's on'y two t' one. Th' odds are gettin' smaller all th' time."

He moved past two empty stores, slipped from doorway to doorway, lingered briefly in the second one and eyed the sprawled-out figure in the street.

"Big feller, awright," he muttered. "There's somethin' about 'im that kinda r'minds me o' that Tex Murray. Wonder if it is."

He loosened his gun in its holster. He was some fifteen feet from the "K. C." He crept across the intervening space and dropped down against the wall of the café, following it to the rear. There was a back door; he tried it and was not surprised to find it locked. Two saddled horses a little farther away turned their heads, looked at him and whinnied, and he cursed them under his breath. There was a lariat hanging from the saddle horn of one of the horses, and he snatched it off quickly. He uncoiled it, whirled it, then backed away and looked upward. The lariat spun skyward and the noose opened above a chimney. When Canavan jerked his arm downward, the noose settled and snapped tight around the chimney. Hand over hand Canavan went up the rope. He swung himself close to the building and inched his way toward an upper-floor window. Halfway up he stopped; his arms were tired and he was panting. After a brief respite, he went on again, finally dragging himself up to the window.

He twisted his leg around the rope, slammed against the building, reached up, got his fingers under the window and pushed it up. A minute later he was straddling the window sill. He swung himself over it and into the room. Quickly he looked about him. It was a poorly furnished room; there was a backless chair in one corner, and a pair of dirty, battered boots standing beside it; a single cot occupied the length of the far wall. There was no bedding on the cot, nothing but a worn, soiled-looking blanket heaped on it. Canavan made a wry face; there was a musty smell about the place. He tiptoed across the room to the door, turned the knob, opened the door the least bit and peered out. There was a dim hallway, and opening on it were two other rooms with closed doors. He studied them for a moment, then he slipped out.

He edged his way up to the first door and listened; there was no sound from behind the closed door, and he moved away to the last one. He bent down to the level of the keyhole; he straightened up presently, turned the knob, and the door opened. Cautiously he poked his head inside. The room was completely vacant, and he stepped back, closed the door and tiptoed to the head of the stairway. He crouched there and peered over the banister; he heard voices below and he nodded grimly. He jerked out his gun, gripped it tightly and started down the stairs. The wooden step was warped and it squeaked beneath him and he cursed it. There was a sudden scurrying about in the café below. He drew a deep breath.

"Wa—al," he said to himself, "here goes!"

He went plunging down the stairs. As he reached the lower floor, he threw himself sideways, firing as he twisted away. He caught a glimpse of a tall man with a rifle, and a shorter man with a half-raised Colt. Canavan dropped behind a table, pulling it down in front of him.

Gunfire rocked the café. Canavan dove behind a second table and snapped two quick shots. Quarles and Fox, backing toward the open doorway, collided with each other but managed to get out of the "K. C." The rifle thundered again. Canavan, swinging away toward the wall, reached it and fired a shot in reply; as he moved again, he stumbled over an overturned chair and his gun exploded. The bullet shattered the front window and it fell out. Another equally errant shot, fired from outside the café, smashed the row of bottles on the shelf behind the bar, and whiskey spouted and spewed over the mirror, running down the wall. Canavan came skidding across the café floor, slammed into the bar, dropped down behind it and fired into the street. Hastily now he crammed fresh cartridges into his gun, arose, dashed to the doorway and bolted out. He got a blurred view of Quarles nearing the other side of the street, and he fired at him, and pulled back again inside for a moment. He peered out presently and stared with widening eyes; Quarles was down on his hands and knees. Canavan stepped outside. There was no sign of Matt Fox.

Canavan held his fire. He watched Quarles warily. Slowly, evidently painfully, Quarles forced himself up. He braced himself, his legs spread wide apart. He made no attempt to pick up the rifle which now lay at his feet. Instead he sought to draw the holstered gun that hung at his right hip; finally he managed to pull it out. He raised his head, looked at Canavan and grinned. He flipped his left hand casually, as if in greeting, suddenly jerked his gun hand upward. The two men fired as one. Canavan's hat was torn off his head; he fired twice more and

Quarles dropped his gun, stumbled blindly, stopped and suddenly pitched forward on his face.

Canavan dashed into the street and kicked Quarles's gun out of reach. The sprawled-out body he had seen earlier was less than a dozen feet beyond Quarles's. Canavan bent down and turned the man over on his back. He nodded when he saw the man's face. It was Tex Murray. A gun barked far down the street and he turned quickly. Matt Fox was standing at the entrance to an alley, firing at someone in the doorway of the bank directly across the street. Canavan raced down the street. A rifle boomed and Fox staggered out of the alley. He dropped his gun and turned slowly as though he simply intended to walk away. The rifle roared again, deep-throatedly, and Fox fell. Two men emerged from the bank; the taller one, Colonel Wynn, carried a half-raised rifle. The shorter man looked up the street, spied Canavan and waved.

"We got 'im!" he yelled. "We got 'im!"

Beth Richards came racing around the house as Canavan thundered up.

"Johnny!" she screamed joyfully.

He pulled up abruptly, fairly leaped out of the saddle and caught her in his arms.

"You're—you're all right?" she panted.

"An' how, honey!"

She bowed her head, pillowed it on his chest and clung to him tightly.

"Hey!"

"Yes?" she asked without raising her head.

"Did you know that Colonel Wynn was a judge b'sides bein' a banker?"

"No," she said. There was a sob in her voice.

"Wa—al, if you'll kinda look up at a feller, mebbe he'll tell you somethin' interestin'."

"I—I left my handkerchief inside."

"Oh!" he said and whipped out his own. "Here."

She wiped her eyes. Slowly she raised her head.

"Colonel Wynn an' th' others'll be here soon," he said. "You ain't got more'n ten minutes t' fix y'self up, y'know."

"Fix myself up?"

"Uh-huh. Th' Colonel says he c'n marry us, an' I tol' 'im we'd be ready f'r 'im th' minute he got here."

"Oh!" she said and stepped away from him. "Oh, my goodness! Ten minutes?"

"That's right," he said gravely.

"But, Johnny—"

"You don't need even one minute," she heard him say. "You're just th' way I want you—just th' way you are right now."

There was a loud clatter of galloping, pounding hoofs. As they turned, a group of hard-riding horsemen dashed into view. They came thundering up to them, reined in and swung themselves out of their saddles. Henry Comerford was the first man to dismount; now he came scampering up to them.

"The stolen bank money's been found!" he panted excitedly. "Right after you left Logan, a troop of Rangers rode into town. They searched the 'K. C.' and found the money in the cellar."

"Swell!"

Comerford laughed.

"That isn't all. They killed or captured every one of Quarles's men," he added.

"Then Logan's gonna be a good place t' live in."

"That's the way I figured it, too. The Ranger captain told me all about you, how you'd resigned from the Rangers and how the governor had talked you into accepting one last assignment, the job of cleaning up Logan. Well, you've done your job, Johnny. Logan wants to offer you another one. It's yours for as long as you want it. Frankly, I think it should be an easy one now. And with Logan peopled by decent home-loving citizens, it should be an ideal place for a man to bring up a family. What d'you say, Johnny?"

Canavan smiled and shook his head.

"No," he answered quietly. "My dad's got a big place an' he's gettin' on in years. I've got t' be gettin' back t' him. B'sides, I was born and raised in Texas an' I'd kinda like t' have my kids—"

There was a tug at his sleeve.

"Johnny."

He turned his head and looked down quickly.

"Colonel Wynn is waiting," Beth said.

"Oh!" he said. He smiled, took Beth's hand in his and squared his shoulders. "Awright, Colonel, I'm ready!"